PREGNANT BY THE SHEIKH

OLIVIA GATES

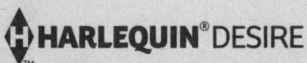

HARLEQUIN® DESIRE

Recycling programs
for this product may
not exist in your area.

ISBN-13: 978-0-373-73376-7

Pregnant by the Sheikh

Printed in U.S.A.

"You want an heir?"

Jen heard her voice as if coming from someone else.

"Yes. An heir you'll give me."

The room started spinning. "I knew you'd have a price for helping me, but I never thought it would be that."

"What did you think it would be? Yourself?"

Yes, she'd thought he'd want an affair. But she wouldn't have considered that a price. It would have been a reward.

His brooding gaze captured her wandering eyes. "I never bargain for sexual favors."

"No, you'd just have to make your desire known and women would line up to give you your heir."

"I am making my desire known. To the only woman I ever considered for the role."

"Why me?"

He gathered her tighter against his incredible heat and hardness. "Because you're in my arms, within an hour of meeting. The attraction between us combusted the moment I saw you, and it's been raging higher ever since."

She wanted to wind herself around him, to forget everything and act on the need burning them up.

For the first time in her life she didn't have control. And she loved it.

* * *

Pregnant by the Sheikh is part of The Billionaires of Black Castle series: Only their dark pasts could lead these men to the light of true love.

* * *

If you're on Twitter,
tell us what you think of Harlequin Desire!
#harlequindesire

Dear Reader,

In the third book of The Billionaires of Black Castle series, it was great to again write one of the heroes I like best—a sheikh. And Numair wasn't any sheikh. He was one who'd been robbed of his heritage and was now back to claim everything he'd been deprived of...at any cost. He was also the leader of the brotherhood he'd forged in the dark years when he and those he'd picked to be his blood brothers had been turned into unstoppable mercenaries.

Now, a most dangerous and powerful billionaire, he comes to the region from where he'd been plucked as a child and thrown into a nightmarish existence, to exact revenge and reclaim his throne. And his key to having both is one particular princess. He vows to make her his, just because she will serve all his purposes.

Then he actually meets her...and any premeditation is incinerated in the conflagration of passion that erupts between them. Soon he reaches an impossible decision: the woman who created a beating heart inside him—the mother of his unborn child—or the goals that fueled his whole life.

What follows is a roller coaster of passion, emotions and angst. I hope you enjoy Numair and Jenan's story as much as I enjoyed writing it!

I love to hear from readers, so please visit my website at oliviagates.com and connect with me at oliviagates@gmail.com, on Facebook at facebook.com/oliviagatesauthor, on Goodreads at goodreads.com/author/show/405461.Olivia_Gates and on Twitter: @OliviaGates.

Thanks for reading,

Olivia Gates

Olivia Gates has always pursued creative passions such as singing and handicrafts. She still does, but only one of her passions grew gratifying enough, consuming enough, to become an ongoing career—writing.

She is most fulfilled when she is creating worlds and conflicts for her characters, then exploring and untangling them bit by bit, sharing her protagonists' every heart-wrenching heartache and hope, their every heart-pounding doubt and trial, until she leads them to an indisputably earned and gloriously satisfying happy ending.

When she's not writing, she is a doctor, a wife to her own alpha male and a mother to one brilliant girl and one demanding Angora cat. Visit Olivia at oliviagates.com.

Books by Olivia Gates

HARLEQUIN DESIRE

Desert Knights

The Sheikh's Redemption
The Sheikh's Claim
The Sheikh's Destiny

Married by Royal Decree

Temporarily His Princess
Conveniently His Princess
Seducing His Princess

The Billionaires of Black Castle

From Enemy's Daughter to Expectant Bride
Scandalously Expecting His Child
Pregnant by the Sheikh

Visit the Author Profile page
at Harlequin.com for more titles.

To Kathryn Falk. Words aren't enough to describe what your unstinting support means to me, and how it has made what I feared might be impossible come true.

One

Jenan Aal Ghamdi watched the man she was getting engaged to flit among throngs of congratulators—and almost barfed. Again.

It never failed. Every time she looked at him, hell, every time she thought of him, nausea overpowered her. It was a testament to her self-control that she hadn't thrown up all over him yet.

The one thing stopping her from giving in to the compulsion was the stronger aversion to rejoining that tragic farce of an engagement celebration. It had taken her over an hour to escape the hordes of prying—and pitying—guests and take refuge at the far end of the massive ballroom. She'd managed to slink away unnoticed only because she'd refused to wear the getup her "fiancé" had sent her. He'd wanted to flaunt his newly massive wealth and drape his "acquisition" in an oppressively ornate costume complete with scaffolding. With the ton of clashing jewelry he'd provided, she would have glittered with the power of ten disco balls. As it was, in her most obscure and suitably mournful matte black evening gown, she now blended into the darkness of the ballroom's periphery. It was a minuscule victory, but with her expectations reduced to nil, anything counted now.

Retreating farther away from everyone's line of sight, she started breathing normally again. And a surreal sense of detachment descended on her yet again. It was as if none of this was really happening to her but to someone else. As if this was some ridiculous dream she was confident would fade into nothingness the moment she woke up.

The artificial serenity lasted only moments before the illusion splintered and reality crashed over her again, with another wave of queasiness.

She was really getting engaged to Hassan Aal Ghaanem!

The man who happened to be the king of Saraya, who held Zafrana, his neighboring desert kingdom and her homeland, hostage.

No, she wasn't getting engaged to the man, she was being bartered to him. Sold. Tonight felt like the beginning of the end of her life as she knew it. The end of her life, period. Whatever came after marrying him wouldn't be considered life. Not in her book.

But though this fate was inescapable, she'd still refused to have this reception in Saraya, or even in Zafrana. It had been another empty triumph when he'd relented and agreed to hold it here, in her New York City stomping grounds.

The city had been her home for the past twelve years. It would stop being so once she started serving her life sentence as Hassan's wife. But she'd refused to go back to that region to be buried there for the rest of her life a second before she absolutely had to. She'd fled, determined to never return, except for fleeting visits, which had been few and very brief.

But she'd been regretting her insistence since the moment she'd seen that man's over-the-top arrangements. If there was anything more abhorrent to her than Hassan himself right now, it was being the center of attention in such an extravagant, overexposed event.

If this party had been held in their homelands, it wouldn't have gotten any coverage, what with the privacy measures imposed by the ruling class. But in the heart of New York City and in such a venue with all those high-profile attendees, this engagement party would be all over the worldwide media. Which taught her not to struggle while sinking in quicksand. Her attempt to assert herself had only made her sink deeper in this mess.

But teaching her a lesson about defying him hadn't been Hassan's objective in arranging this spectacle. The man considered nothing but himself. And as the king of a recently prosperous kingdom—now that King Mohab Aal Ghaanem of Jareer was giving Saraya 30 percent of the new kingdom's massive oil wealth—Hassan Aal Ghaanem had been on a splurging spree after decades of being held back by his kingdom's limited finances.

So here they were, in the Terrace Room at The Plaza, where many a legendary celebrity had held prominent events. After all, Hassan considered himself on par with those people.

Any other time, she would have appreciated the almost five-thousand-square-foot ballroom that had been restored to its early 1900s grandeur. When she'd been here before, the painted ceilings, cathedral-like arches and elaborate pillars leading to its wraparound gallery had transported her to the Renaissance, while the original crystal chandeliers, wall paneling and carpeting had added a golden age refinement to the classical setting. Being here now, for this horrendous occasion, it felt like the setting of her life's worst nightmare. It literally was.

Tearing her gaze away from the five hundred guests that filled the ballroom to capacity, her eyes fell to her bare hands. She'd refused to accept the priceless pieces from Saraya's royal jewelry to be her *shabkah*—what literally meant "binding." She was damned if she'd wear his shackles for all to see…

"Are you sure about this, Jen?"

The soft voice, barely audible above the Sarayan celebratory songs blaring over the sound system, sent a spasm through her chest with its melancholy. Zeena, her baby half sister. If anyone was feeling as bad as she was about this whole thing, it was her.

She turned to her, her lips crooking in an attempt at lightness. "Oh, I am, Zee. I'm sure there's no other way out of the mess Father and Zafrana are in but for me to marry that old goat."

And that mess wasn't a recent development, but one with decades-long roots. It was also one she had an indirect hand in.

It had started when her father, Khalil Aal Ghamdi, had found himself on Zafrana's throne after King Zayd, his second cousin, had died, with him as his closest male relative. Pushed into a position he'd been unsuited for, her father, a dreamer and an artist, had been unable to become a man of state and had been led astray by many an unqualified or malicious counselor.

When she'd returned to Zafrana after graduating from Cornell University with degrees in economics and business administration, she'd seen how her father's imprudent policies had led to the kingdom's steady deterioration. She'd tried to guide him, but his entourage's opposition had been vicious. They'd undone everything she'd accomplished until she'd found herself with only two choices: dedicate her life to fighting that vicious cycle or withdraw from the battle and flee the whole region, where the very way of life was anathema to her. She'd chosen to give up and leave.

As a result of her withdrawal, Zafrana was now cripplingly in debt...to Saraya. And Hassan was now poised to annex the kingdom through a marriage of state. Which, her father had informed her, was the only way to save Zafrana. Knowing the depths of the debt, she believed him.

"But you can't marry him. He's—he's *old*!"

At Zeena's horrified lament, Jen huffed in bitter irony. "Yeah, I noticed. Hard to miss when your prospective groom is as old as your own father, and reprehensible to boot. Not to mention heinously boring. And to think when the marriage of state was first proposed, I point-blank refused to marry Najeeb."

Zeena's honey-brown eyes flared with hope. "Maybe it's not too late to take your refusal back! I know you love Najeeb like a brother, but if you have to marry anyone, at least he's a great guy. And a real hunk. You might end up loving him...*that* way!"

Jen regarded her seventeen-year-old stunning beauty of a sister and remembered again why she was doing this. She sighed. "You think I wouldn't have grabbed that option if it was still on the table? But Najeeb was as adamant in refusing to marry me just to serve his father's political ambitions. Then he left to places unknown on another of his globe-trotting humanitarian missions. That's why Hassan decided he'd marry me himself."

"Doesn't this man have a shred of decency? He's actually two years older than Father!"

"He actually considers he's done the noble thing, offering his oldest son and crown prince first, and that it was my and Najeeb's refusals that made him resort to this option. He feels quite righteous, I assure you."

Zeena looked on the verge of crying again. She'd been looking like that ever since she'd heard the news. But she was clearly past the shock phase and into the bargaining one.

"But if you really have to go through with it—" she paused to shudder "—maybe it won't be for long."

"You're hoping he'll soon drop dead and release me from my life sentence?" She shook her head at yet more proof of how young and naive her sister was. "Zee, darling, I know anyone over forty is ancient to you. Hell, I'm only thirty, and you make me feel old whenever you're shocked I do stuff you think reserved for only 'young' people. But Hassan is a very robust sixty-five, and I expect him to live another healthy, obnoxious thirty years."

Zeena clearly couldn't imagine that terrible fate, or could, and it horrified her. Her tears finally flowed, her voice breaking. "At least tell me it will only be for show."

Jen sighed again, not knowing what to tell her sister. Their father had mumbled such an assurance, but she figured it had to be what he'd told himself so he wouldn't feel even guiltier about sacrificing her. Hassan already had a chokehold over Zafrana's resources and assets, but in their region, blood mattered far more than money when it came to political power. This marriage had to produce an heir, one who'd become her father's, too, for Hassan to acquire all the power he wanted over Zafrana. Only through such an heir could Hassan rule Zafrana during her father's lifetime, then fully annex it in the event of his death, once his heir became king, and Hassan became regent until said heir came of age. Hassan sure had his ducks in a row. And she was the first one he had sitting just where he wanted her.

Zeena must have read the truth in her resigned eyes, as her tears flowed faster. But she still tried again. "If all he has over Father and Zafrana are debts, maybe we can find someone to pay them off. Like the other royals in the region. Surely great men and kings like King Kamal and King Mohab will help."

Jen shook her head, wanting to end this. "I approached everyone with power in the region myself, but all kings Kamal, Mohab, Amjad and Rashid could do was try to make Hassan relinquish those debts to them, and he refused. Without resorting to drastic measures, there's nothing they can do."

"Why won't they employ those measures? This *is* drastic!"

"It isn't as easy as that, Zee. These men owe it to their own kingdoms not to involve them in other nations' conflicts. And since the influx of oil money, Hassan now has major foreign allies whose interests lie with Saraya and who'd take exception if the other kingdoms enforced embargos on it, or initiated a bigger conflict with it. Also, with the tribal nature of the region, those kings have family alliances with Saraya, making things even more complicated."

She knew each king wanted to tear Hassan apart with his bare hands. But those hands were tied by so many protocols. They were forced to accept any form of peaceful resolution, even if they itched for something extreme. Said *peaceful resolution* was now her, and her hopefully fertile womb.

"So this is for real?" Zeena asked. "There's no way out?"

"No."

Her succinct response fell like a blow on Zeena, rocking her on her feet. The next second, Zeena's arms were convulsing around her, and her tears were wetting her bosom.

Jen's eyes filled, too. She hadn't shed tears since her mother's death when she was seven. But she'd never been able to bear her baby sisters' distress.

Apart from loving her most in the world, Zeena and Fayza looked up to her. Her every success had been a triumph to them. She'd been their role model, her life one they hoped to model theirs after. Zeena wasn't only weeping for Jen's derailed future, but for a loss of hope in her own.

But that was why Jen had agreed to this marriage. To protect her sisters' futures.

She'd only told Zeena there was no way out so she wouldn't compound her distress with guilt. For there certainly was a way out for Jen had she wanted to take it. She could have told her father and Hassan to take flying jumps off their respective kingdoms' tallest skyscraper. But she hadn't. For two reasons.

The first and lesser reason was that she couldn't stand aside and let their father be humiliated and hurt. She loved him, in spite of his weaknesses, felt even more protective of him because of them. She knew he shouldn't have become king, that it continued to be an unbearable burden. But fate had conspired to put him on the throne, and it had been the one thing that had appeased many a tribe at the time. He'd sacrificed his own desires for Zafrana's. This current mess was not solely his fault. In her pursuit of independence, her career and immigration to the United States, she'd stopped following the developments in Zafrana, until things had deteriorated beyond resolution. The internal situation was now so volatile, if the major tribes didn't get a solution soon and with their interests finally threatened by Saraya's impending takeover, civil war would erupt.

But the major reason she'd agreed to the marriage remained her sisters. Even if she'd been able to leave her father and her people to a doom they'd caused, she couldn't leave Zeena and Fayza to a fate they hadn't brought on themselves. If Hassan couldn't have her, he'd ask for one of her sisters. And their father would be forced to comply.

But they were nothing like her. They were too young, too sheltered and too inexperienced in life and with men. They didn't have the power of another nationality and the protection of personal wealth. If Jen left, neither of her sisters would be able to resist being shoved into this marriage. Zeena would crumble, and the two-years-older Fayza would do something drastic.

So it was up to her to protect them. She had to marry that power-grabbing old man and save them. And along with them, her whole family and kingdom.

She hugged the sobbing Zeena tighter, kissed the top of her head soothingly. "Don't worry about me, Zee. You know me. I'm a survivor, a winner, and I'll find a way to…to…"

Words and thoughts petered away. The whole scene in front of her blurred, then disappeared. Nothing remained but a man. The most magnificent male she'd ever laid eyes on…

"To what?"

Jen started at the question, blinked as if coming out of a trance. For seconds she couldn't remember where she was, why she and Zeena were sharing this fervent hug and why her baby sister was looking up at her with such entreaty.

Then noise and lights and movements and memories started to register again. But her senses remained trained on the man as he stood at the ballroom's wide-open doors, surveying it with all the somberness of a general studying a battlefield. He filled her awareness, the sheer force of his presence nullifying everything else. As if he had some kind of gravity well that nothing could resist or escape.

Then he moved, and the crowd parted for him, seemingly unable to withstand being in his path. It felt as if he had a spotlight trained on him, illuminating him even as he dipped in areas of shadow. What else explained why he looked more vivid, more in focus than anyone else who was dozens of feet closer?

"Who's *that*?"

She blinked again as she forced her eyes back to her sister. Zeena had followed her entranced gaze to the mystery man and was staring at him openmouthed. So he had the same effect on her. Of course he did. He had everyone around mesmerized.

It seemed so weird that she didn't know who he was, since she felt she…recognized him.

Exhaling at her inexplicable reactions and thoughts, she shrugged. "I have no idea."

An assessing expression came into Zeena's eyes as she let her go, before impishness suddenly replaced anguish on her face. "Want me to go find out?"

Jen raised one eyebrow. "And how would you do that?"

"I'll walk right up to him, introduce myself as the sister of the bride and just ask."

Jen winced at the word *bride*, but waved dismissively. "Thanks, darling, but you probably wouldn't be able to move, let alone speak, if you come within talking distance of him."

Zeena looked back at the man who kept coming closer to their hideout and sighed. "Yeah, I'd probably turn to stone if he even looked at me."

So even Zeena with her limited experience with the world in general and men in particular felt the impact of this man. As for herself, she'd been exposed to some of the most powerful men on earth in over a decade of studies, travels and public and private work, and she knew beyond a doubt that this man was exceptional among even those. More than that. He was one of a kind. The way he affected her was unprecedented. And that was from afar, when he was completely unaware of her.

Suddenly, knowing who he was became the most important thing to her. Before she led a mockery of a life dictated by everyone else's interests, she was due for one thing all her own. What better than to indulge her unstoppable curiosity about this man? After all, where did being perfectly responsible and in control lead her? But then, why should she even need a reason? She was just going to find out who he was, not have a fling with him.

Yeah, right, as if such a force of nature would look in her direction, even if he weren't here attending her engagement party.

But she would do this, for herself. Even if for some reason she felt the simple action of discovering his identity would have some unpredictable and serious consequences.

Straightening, she rolled her shoulders, as if readying herself for a fight. "I'll do it. I'll go investigate."

Before she strode away, Zeena's hand on her forearm stopped her. "Just be careful. This guy is radiating something fierce."

Jen's gaze went to him again, and she nodded. "That's called power. The unadulterated form."

"I guess. But he just feels—" Zeena looked suddenly uncomfortable "—dangerous."

Jen's lips curved as she repeated to her sister what she'd just been thinking. "Darling, I'm just going to find out who he is, not have a fling with him."

Zeena gave an embarrassed giggle as Jen swept her velvet cheek in one last reassuring caress before striding away.

As she rejoined the crowd, heading for the one most likely to know who that man was, Jen exhaled a ragged breath. For Zeena was so right.

She had no doubt this demigod was very dangerous. Deadly. But that only made her desire to find out everything about him even more overpowering.

She zeroed in on Jameel Aal Hashem, her five-years-younger maternal cousin, a walking encyclopedia of social gossip and celebrity news. She'd bet her mystery man hadn't escaped her cousin's all-encompassing curiosity.

And she was right. Before she could even ask Jameel, he pointed out the stranger in a fit of ecstatic excitement.

After gushing about how he couldn't believe *he* was here, Jameel told her who he was. Numair Al Aswad.

And how fitting that name was. He was indeed as majestic and sleek and powerful as his namesake. He *was* actually known by the English version of his name: the Black Panther of Black Castle Enterprises.

Now that she knew his name, she knew far more about him than Jameel possibly could. Since she'd become deeply involved in the world of business, anywhere she'd turned there it had been, the global corporation he'd founded that was shaping the market in every major field that made the world go round.

As the senior partner, Numair was a leader among the gods of science, finance and technology responsible for Black Castle Enterprises' staggering success, and one of the most individually rich and powerful men on the planet. And now she'd found out that he was also the sexiest thing to ever walk the earth.

But not much was known about his personal life. Only that he came from Damhoor, a kingdom in her region, but had immigrated to the United States in his childhood, and his parents were long dead. As far as she knew, he'd never been married.

Then at one point, as Jameel joined her in openly drooling over the man, Numair turned and looked straight at them.

At *her*.

His gaze slammed into her own with the force of a lightning bolt. Feeling as if it had fried her brain, nothing was left in her mind but alarm.

Had he felt her staring at him?

Before her stalled breathing could restart, people moved in front of her, severing the electrified visual contact.

Shaky with relief and disappointment at once, she murmured something to Jameel and hurried away, unable to risk being in Numair's crosshairs again.

Secure that Hassan hadn't bothered to look for her, she maneuvered around the few people who recognized her to rush back to her retreat. She wanted to continue watching Numair from its safety. The memory of savoring his magnificence would be what she'd remember from this wretched night.

As she reached her previous vantage point, another jolt hit her again. It was fiercer this time, making her stumble and drop her purse. Cursing when it opened on impact, spilling its contents, she crouched to retrieve them…and felt as if the place was plunged into darkness. The next second, she knew why. It was the massive figure towering over her, seeming to block out the whole world. She didn't need to look up to see who it was. The current that now mercilessly arced through her told her who it was.

Numair.

As her chest filled to bursting with erratic heartbeats, he dropped to his haunches before her. Before she could raise her eyes to his, his hands, cool and calloused, brushed hers and zapped her with another thousand volts as he took the purse from her limp grasp and put everything back in it, his every move the essence of control and elegance.

As he handed it back to her, she mustered enough volition and looked up…and lost what remained of her compromised balance. Only the hand that shot out to support her stopped her from flopping back on her ass.

Finding herself inches from him was as heart-stopping, literally, as finding herself face-to-face with his predator namesake. All that lethal power coiled and simmering under the polished, perfect veneer of savage beauty.

She now realized she'd gotten it wrong before. He was no demigod. This was a full-fledged god, one who ruled over a whole pantheon of deities. A desert god in specific, forged from its heat and harshness, from its mystery and moodiness and magnificence. He might not have lived long in her region, but his heritage was carved in his every line.

And *carved* was an accurate word. Every inch of him seemed to have been hewn by some divine force. His all-black formal silk suit and shirt clung to a body she had no doubt was solid, chiseled muscle. The clothes offered not an inch of padding to the breadth of his shoulders and chest, no accentuation to the hardness of his abdomen and thighs or the sparseness of his waist and hips. This was the full potential of the species realized, a powerhouse of virility and manliness.

And that was before she took in the details of his face. From a luxurious mane of raven silk that would reach almost to his shoulders when freed, to stunning emerald eyes that seemed to radiate a hypnosis, to sensual lips and polished teak–colored skin spread taut against a bone structure to tear heartstrings over, he was breathtaking.

Then he was pulling her up to her feet as he uncoiled to his full height, and for the first time ever she felt dwarfed. She stood six feet in three-inch heels, and he still towered over her by what appeared to be half a foot.

Then he did something that once again made her heart hammer as if it was trying to ram out of her chest. He raised a hand and swept back the swath of hair that had cascaded over her face, ensnaring one strand, rubbing it between his fingers.

"You hate being here."

No preliminaries. Just…*bam*. Of course he would follow no rules. It made it even worse that his voice was like darkest velvet gliding over her every nerve. Did he have to sound mouthwatering, too?

Without meaning to, she found herself responding, as if under the effect of a truth serum. "I do."

He nodded, as if he'd already been certain, but approved

her corroboration. "This—" he swept the whole scene in a disdainful flick "—is unworthy of your tolerance or your presence."

She had to force the mouth that kept dropping open closed. "Sometimes we're forced to put up with much, for the sake of what's more important than our own preferences or what we think we're worthy of."

His lips and eyes hardened, clearly disapproving. "Nothing is more important than your preferences. And your worth is not a matter of opinion. Only the best is good enough for you. The only thing you must always expect and get."

The heart that seemed to have taken permanent residence in her throat expanded at his praise. Even if it was empty hyperbole, it sounded fantastic coming from him.

"Uh, thanks...but you don't really know anything about me. And it's clear you have no idea who I am."

That dismissing wave again. "The moment I laid eyes on you, I knew everything I need to know about you. As for your identity, that makes no difference to who you really are, what you truly deserve."

"Oh, believe me, it does."

"Because you're Jenan Aal Ghamdi, and this is supposed to be your engagement party?"

He knew who she was. And it didn't seem to make a difference to him.

His next words made that clear beyond a doubt. "It's all quite irrelevant to me. And should be to you, too. You don't want to be here. But you want to be with me."

"I—I do?"

"Yes. As much as I want to be with you." His words were dripping in arrogant certainty. From another man, it would have been offensive. She'd handed other men their asses over *way* less. From him, though, it was just right. He had a right to such supreme self-assurance.

His eyes flared in the dimness as they caressed her half-open lips before settling back on her no doubt shell-shocked eyes. "Let me take you away from this farce. I'm the only one who can give you everything you need."

She gaped up at him. Was she so traumatized by the idea of marrying Hassan that she was having a wish-fulfillment hallucination? Creating this god of a man and making it so she'd had the same instant, inexorable effect on him that he'd had on her?

But nothing she could conjure could be as outlandishly incredible as him. No, he was real. He had really followed her here, and he really was offering…offering…

She didn't know exactly what he was offering. But anything coming from him sounded better than any fantasy she'd ever had. And more impossible.

Her situation might be irrelevant to him, but to her…

Suddenly, everything inside her hit Pause. In seconds, an urge took her over. A plan. It was rash, probably crazy, but it was all she could think of anymore.

This man was even more powerful than the monarchs she'd approached for help. His power was also unbridled by any of their tribal and political shackles, and it was more than enough to resolve Zafrana's crisis without her sacrificing herself to this barbaric ritual of an arranged marriage. Of course, a man like him wouldn't help out of the goodness of his heart.

She had a feeling he didn't have one.

But if he was as interested in her as he seemed to be, they might come to an understanding.

Even if she couldn't imagine he was that interested, he'd help with something that major. As a businesswoman, she was used to taking risks. The worst that could happen was he'd decline and just walk away. But since the stakes were so high and he was that tempting, she'd risk far more than his mere rejection.

Before she could think again, she said it out loud, making it too late to back down. "There *is* something I need."

"Anything."

His instant, unqualified statement gave her the last shove of courage she needed to make her request.

"I need you to get me out of marrying Hassan."

Two

"Done."

Numair watched the impact of his one-word answer widening Jenan Aal Ghamdi's magnificent eyes, spreading a deeper peach blush across the sculpted elegance of her cheekbones.

He was again almost overwhelmed by the need to trace that delectable color that kept surging across her face, the testament to his effect on this irresistible creature. And to luxuriate in every line of her masterpiece features, then drag her to him and taste each one before settling on her lush, dewy lips and devouring them.

It again baffled him, his response to her, the intensity, the immediacy of it. This was unprecedented, inexplicable. Yet it was most opportune. He'd come here for her after all.

He'd come knowing everything about her from the day she'd been born to the moment before he'd seen her. He'd compiled a dossier on her thicker than any he'd ever had on a quarry. From photographs, he'd noted her esthetic symmetry, but he hadn't had any response to it, as usual.

Then he'd seen her in the flesh, and all thoughts of swallowing the bitter pill of necessity had been decimated by the thunderbolt of his response to her. Compulsions he'd never even imagined had taken him over the moment he'd laid eyes on her across the distance.

No. They'd done so even before he had. He'd *felt* her first.

Not that he'd realized what it had been he'd felt when a charge of energy had zapped him as soon as he'd entered this ballroom. He'd told himself it must have been a surge of resolve, obliterating any aversion to being here, to launching his mission. Those sensations had strengthened with each step he'd taken until he'd become certain it wasn't internal, but a response to another person. A woman. Though he'd never felt anything like that toward one, the awareness he'd felt had been definitely…sensual.

Once sure of that, he hadn't wanted to find the source of the disturbance. It would have been self-sabotaging to make contact with someone who'd triggered such an aberrant reaction in him when he was here in pursuit of a specific woman.

Then that beacon of sensations had moved, and before he could rein himself in, his gaze had been dragged toward it. And he'd found himself looking straight into her eyes. The heart that never faltered and barely sped under extreme conditions, that he almost never felt at all, had dropped a few beats before it had started thundering. It continued to do so.

As their gazes had meshed, so much had collided inside him. Disbelief, wonder, elation and a dozen other things. His target was the same woman who'd had this inexplicable influence on him. He hadn't even thought what his mission would be like, but had been bound on seeing it through regardless. But this presented what he hadn't even considered a possibility. That it would be enjoyable, even pleasurable.

Then he'd followed her, no longer out of calculation but compulsion. Everything he'd said and done since had been spontaneous. And real. One thing had been driving him, the one thing he was certain of.

He wanted her.

Then she'd shocked him yet again when she'd given him the means to the very thing he was here to achieve. Stopping her marriage to Hassan Aal Ghaanem.

But since he'd let go of all premeditation, he hadn't even hesitated. His response had been instantaneous.

The moment it had left his lips, he'd wished it back. This wasn't how he'd intended this to go. He'd intended to maneuver her, to reel her in slowly, to spoil Hassan's marriage arrangement by seducing his bride-to-be and claiming her for himself. What he'd just offered wouldn't serve his purpose.

But he couldn't take it back. Not when she'd looked up at him with such hope and entreaty as she'd made her request.

Nothing remained on her face now but shock. She must have expected him to say just about anything else but his succinct promise.

He watched the smooth column of her throat working, and he hardened all over as he imagined his lips soothing the convulsive movement, swallowing her moans at their origin.

Then in that velvety voice that strummed every male fiber in his body, her husky question validated his assessment of her incredulity. "Just…done?"

That was his cue to add some qualification, to drive his own bargain. But he couldn't bear to think of interrupting the unrehearsed progression of events.

Deciding to let this play out and adjust his direction later, he nodded. "I did say I'd do anything for you. I intend to."

And the strangest thing was, he did. Apart from what he had to gain by intervening, what drove him now was the need to wipe this trapped expression from her face. He'd come here thinking she'd agreed to marry Hassan to have access to his bottomless oil-money resources. While her history painted a picture of an independent, successful woman, he'd known of many such women who preferred being subsidized once the opportunity presented itself. That she'd refused to marry Najeeb, then consented to marry his father had made him think she'd preferred the older man who'd make far less demands, and who'd be far easier to manipulate.

But one look at her had told him that she found Hassan and the idea of marrying him abhorrent on all levels. How she was being forced to enter that marriage, he had no idea yet, but he didn't doubt that she was, and that she was seething with futile rage at having no choice. A choice he would now give her.

Not that she believed he could, not as easily as he'd implied. He saw the flare of hope in her eyes dim with the gloom of reality. "Intentions are one thing, executions are another."

"Not to me. Anything I intend, I execute."

At the certainty in his words, her gaze flickered again. "But surely not *anything*."

He shrugged. "I can do anything I put my mind to. I always have. And I always will."

Her edible lips hung open for moments before a breathy chuckle escaped them. Her every expression and sound inflamed him. Her every inch, even in that unflattering dress, seemed to be exerting an inexorable gravity on his every cell and sense.

She shook her head in dazed humor, and the silky waves of her hair undulated around her shoulders. "You know what? I believe you can. The universe must bend over backward to accommodate you." Her eyes turned serious, and he wished to fast-forward in time to when she'd look up at him with eyes blazing with passion as he rode her to ecstasy. "But don't you want to know what this is all about before you make such a commitment?"

He shrugged again. "All I need to know is that you enlisted my help in escaping a fate I believe is worse than death to you. Whatever needs to be done, I'll do it."

"But you still need to know details, so you can decide what needs to be done."

And he gave in to the urge. He reached out and cupped her face, groaned as her firm softness filled his palm, as her flesh singed him with that perfect storm of chemistry that had erupted between them.

He barely stopped himself from swooping to claim the lips that spilled such an intoxicating gasp at his touch. He groaned. "You can tell me everything you want…in my suite."

His hand melted down her neck and shoulder before it closed over a resilient arm as he turned toward the French doors to lead her outside.

At her rooted unresponsiveness, he frowned. "You do know who I am?"

She had to. She wouldn't have asked what she had from someone else. For who else could she think could thwart a king?

But he was suddenly uncertain she knew. After all, nothing so far had followed any logical projections.

She silently nodded, her eyes still filled with that shell-shocked expression.

He pressed. "You're not sure you can trust me?"

She shook her head, then squeezed her eyes shut. When

she opened them again, they blasted him in an even hotter wave of unconscious sensuality. He barely suppressed a shudder.

But her color had become hectic and her breathing erratic. She swayed unsteadily in his grip.

Suddenly anxious, he asked, "Are you all right?"

She nodded again, then groaned. "Hell, I keep nodding and shaking my head as if I've forgotten how to speak."

His eyes assessed her as he took his hand reluctantly away. "Maybe you don't want to speak to me anymore."

Her cough was incredulous. "You're kidding, right?"

"You tell me. It's clear I'm…agitating you."

"Oh, you are. But it has nothing to do with not trusting you. I *do* trust you."

He surveyed her expression, not sure if he was reading it right. Because even knowing who he was, such conviction should be premature. And she didn't strike him as someone given to making such serious claims lightly.

He gritted his teeth. "You don't need to say what you don't feel to placate me or to be polite. You have no reason to trust me. Yet. But I will give you any guarantees you demand so you'll feel safe with me."

A chuckle burst from her lips. "Oh, you have much to learn about me. When I'm not in my professional mode as a multinational business consultant, I lead with my real opinions first and don't bother asking questions later."

This did feel like the truth. This attitude suited her, and everything he felt from her.

His lips relaxed in response to her infectious smile. "I would have nothing less than the whole truth from you."

"Well, you've come to the right person for that."

"I'll count on it. I have no tolerance for empty etiquette and pulling punches, either."

"Yeah, I noticed. You tell it as it is, in the most shockingly direct way possible. Welcome to the club." She grinned up at him, and he again wondered how he didn't have her pressed into that column at her back and was all over her. She made his condition even worse when she sighed, the sound caressing his every nerve. "But I do trust you. I just know you'd never harm me in any way. And don't ask me how I know that. It has nothing to do with anything I know about you. I just do."

"Then why were you so alarmed about coming to my suite if it didn't occur to you I'd take advantage of you?"

Again that unfettered chuckle. "As if. I bet you bound over women who pursue you begging to be taken advantage of."

"You're not *women*. You're you."

"Even if you consider me different…"

"Not different. Unique."

Her color heightened again with pleasure at what should have been an exaggeration but was anything but. "Even if you do consider me that, I can't imagine other men's weaknesses ever applying to you. You wouldn't prey on anyone weaker."

Her opinion of him had something searingly pleasurable swelling inside him. Yet…"I *felt* your anxiety, your distress. I still feel them."

Something soft and even more hard-hitting than all her previous expressions came into her eyes as she cocked her head at him, her lips quirking. "Hello? You do realize you're the most overwhelming man alive, right? As if that wasn't enough, we broke every rule of personal interaction. Heck, we've already progressed to discussing wedding-busting plans. Excuse me if I'm rattled to my core."

"You don't need to be. I care nothing about rules. Between us those don't exist. And you know it."

"You think I know anything right now? I'm not even sure this is really happening or that you really exist. I only know that nothing has ever come close to hitting me this hard."

"Another thing we share, then. Even before I saw you, you hit me harder than anything ever had."

She scrunched her nose at him in adorable teasing. "Don't *you* say what you don't mean to try to tickle my ego."

His lips twisted, admitting his condition to himself even as he did to her. "I do mean it. Your ego has every right to be rolling on the ground laughing." Her chuckle tinkled like crystal with such genuine pleasure, he had to fist his hands to keep them from grabbing her. But he also needed to resolve this issue. "So were you just surprised I asked you back to my suite?"

That delightful lopsided grin flashed wider again. "Surprised is the understatement of the century. But seriously, I just needed a moment for a reality check. And to breathe. You, sir, are more breath depleting than the most insane roller-coaster ride."

Just then another unprecedented thing happened. His own lips spread with a combination of emotions he didn't recognize. If forced to name them, he'd guess they most approximated delight, indulgence, even tenderness.

His smile had an equal and opposite reaction on her. While everything about her made him hard as steel, she melted against the support of the column at her back.

Her gaze poured hot, glazed reproach over him, making him start to ache, throb. "You should be banned by law from doing that. Everything about you is already overkill. A smile, and *that* kind, too, can cause widespread damage."

His smile only widened as triumph revved inside his chest. "No danger of that, as I have no smiles of any kind for anyone. This is exclusively for you."

"So I'm a target group of one, huh?"

Something tightened in his chest as he heard the word *target* on her lips. What she'd been to him before he'd seen her. Now it suddenly felt wrong.

Oblivious to his thoughts, she gazed up at him with what he now believed *was* trust and…was that admiration, too? "I came here tonight thinking I'd run out of luck for life, but because I met you and you've offered what you have, no matter what the outcome will be, I'd already revised my opinion. But to be the sole recipient of your smile? Talk about my luck making a total turnaround."

Giving in to his compulsion, he tugged her to his side. "I'm willing to talk about anything. Just not here. Come with me?"

She nodded, shyness tingeing her gaze, affecting him more because he knew only he elicited such a reaction from her, and it was genuine, like everything else about her. "Just promise me a chance every now and then to catch my breath."

"Although it's the last thing I want, I'll give you all the time you need to feel at total ease with me."

Her eyes twinkled impishly at him. "I don't think it's humanly possible to feel relaxed around you."

After that first smile, another came easier to him. "Tension works, too. As long as it's the delicious kind."

She sighed dramatically. "I don't know about that. What you provoke is too scalding to be called anything so benign."

Her ready confessions of his effect on her surged through him again with such unstoppable desire. Unable to wait any longer, he swept her outside.

As he had her rushing to keep up with his eager steps, she melted into him, as if she needed his support. Then as he steered her toward the elevators, he felt her tensing against him.

This tightness in his chest returned. "Worried again?"

Her smile brightened once more, becoming whimsical as she shook her head. "You'd never be a threat to me, Sheikh Numair. If I have anything to worry about, it's what an overpowering temptation you are."

Something twisted in his gut when she called him *sheikh*. It sounded…so right.

His arm tightened around her, as if in thanks. "It's only fair, since you're that, and more, to me."

Sharing a smile of expectation with her, feeling as if everything he'd ever wanted was within his grasp, he took her into the elevator.

As Numair held the door open for her, Jen walked past him on legs that at once had the consistency of steel and jelly.

She was really here. In his suite.

Trying to focus on anything besides the feel of him at her back, his scent and heat flooding her senses, she tried to look around.

Though she'd stayed at The Plaza before, it had never been in such a room. The one-of-a-kind Royal Plaza Suite was on a level of magnificence that equaled Zafrana's royal palace. Though with the hard times her homeland had fallen on, the state of the two places couldn't be compared. This suite that sprawled over almost five thousand square feet in the most private area of the legendary hotel, overlooking the most prized views in Manhattan—Fifth Avenue and the Pulitzer Fountain—was impeccably maintained. With its rich decorations, sumptuous textiles and exquisite furnishings, all inspired by the ambiance of the royal court of Louis XV, it was the ultimate in luxury. While Zafrana's royal palace, where she'd grown up, was on its way to becoming dilapidated.

Her gaze strayed back to Numair, and she found herself wondering what his home looked like.

Not that she'd ever find out. Whatever was happening here, whatever he was offering, whatever he wanted in return, she had no illusions it would be anything but transient.

Which she was okay with. Anything she'd have with him, anything he could do for her, would be far more than anything she'd dared dream of an hour ago.

Ya Ullah, had it been only an hour? She felt she'd known him, had been in this state of agitated excitement in his company, forever. It felt like days ago when she'd made her reckless request.

She'd more than half expected he'd shrug and move on. His immediate and unequivocal response had been the last thing she'd expected. And it had shocked the hell out of her.

But what else was new? Everything from the moment she'd laid eyes on him had been one shock after another. And here she was. In his suite. What she'd never done with any man. Not even the man she'd once married. She'd always met any man on her turf. She'd dictated the pace, the rules.

She hadn't even thought of trying to impose those on Numair. Even when he'd made it clear he'd accommodate her every wish. It wasn't because she needed his help or because he'd promised it. He was just…overriding. And for the first time in her life, she loved being swept away, not being in control of herself or the situation. Numair made what should have been a disconcerting experience, to someone as obsessive about autonomy as herself, exhilarating.

His hand once again burned her waist through her dress as he guided her through a succession of vestibules to a massive space hosting a sumptuous ten-seat dining table and a luxurious sitting area.

Stepping away from his electrifying touch, she sought the refuge of the grand piano at the far corner. Once behind it and taking in the whole scene with him at its center, she felt herself stumble out of the surreal state she'd plunged into.

Numair might have admitted her equal effect on him, but would he consider it equally her right to follow her instincts as it was his? She did trust him not to make any move she didn't invite, but she suddenly didn't trust he'd view this whole thing as she did. Could he be so progressive he wouldn't hold it against her and change his treatment of her?

Well, if he wasn't, it would be his loss, and she'd be well rid of him. As she had been of her ex.

Striving for an even tone, she asked, "Are you in New York to attend the reception?"

Those amazing emerald-like eyes of his glittered. "I wasn't invited, no."

"So you heard royals from your region were having an engagement celebration at your hotel and you simply decided to investigate?"

"Something like that."

She'd have to be satisfied with that, because he didn't seem about to elaborate. Not that it mattered why he happened to be there. What mattered was whether he could truly help her.

Before she could reintroduce the subject, he came around the piano. "I detect a severe drop in temperature since we entered the suite. Having second thoughts after all?"

His voice had deepened, calmed, as if soothing a skittish mare. He reached for her hand that lay fisted on the black, polished surface of the piano. His hand was big enough to lose hers in, tough enough it could pulverize brick. Yet the gentleness with which he coaxed her hand open, the consideration in his eyes as he surveyed her no doubt tense face, suddenly made her ashamed of her surge of doubt.

Squeezing her eyes in contrition, she groaned, "I guess I got a bit paranoid."

He frowned. "Were you worried that your trust in me was unsubstantiated, and I'd do something against your will once I got you here?"

She shook her head vigorously, needing him to know this was something she'd never suspect. "Not that. I just worried you'd change your…attitude."

"Like men usually do, once they think they've gotten their objectives and no longer need to hide their nasty natures and double-standard convictions?"

From the way his gorgeous lips thinned, she knew if such men crossed his path, they'd regret it for life. He did have that protector/punisher vibe going.

She wished he'd let this go but knew he wouldn't. This man needed to know everything, to have a tight handle on every situation. He'd probe until she spilled everything that had crossed her mind in those moments of unease.

She sighed. "Men are like that to one degree or another in my experience, but mainly men from my region, yes."

One dauntingly arched eyebrow rose. "Are all men chauvinists there?"

"Double standards *are* the general stance, perpetrated by women even more than men. Anyone, especially a woman, who dares flaunt cultural rules and restrictions becomes stigmatized, no matter how modern everyone looks on the surface."

"Why did you fear I'd be like them? I was born in your region, but I was not raised there."

"Indoctrination happens at a very early age. It takes very progressive families and especially mothers not to imprint their children with the worst of the culture. In general, men there are raised to have very cruel opinions of women whom they perceive as 'loose.'"

"And you thought my early programming would resurface, and I'd judge you for coming up here with me?"

"It was a passing thought, okay? An ingrained reaction that really has nothing to do with you."

"But it wasn't ingrained in you because of the general state of affairs in your homeland. It was out of personal experience, wasn't it?"

She'd been right. He wouldn't rest until he had the whole truth. She sighed again. "How much do you know about me? You clearly investigated me before crashing the reception."

He guided her to the nearest couch, pulled her down on it with him. "Investigations provide only broad lines that can be interpreted in different ways that can all turn out to be wrong. You tell me what's accurate."

Shuddering as his power and warmth encompassed her, she leaned against the dark brown velvet couch. She hoped she didn't look as swooning as she felt as she gazed up at him.

"I am the very definition of *loose* in my region. From leaving my family at eighteen to live in another country, to supporting myself ever since, to making success and autonomy my life goal, to being a divorcée who hasn't returned home in penance, seeking the shelter of her family and the forgiveness of society, I'm the cautionary tale mothers tell their little daughters. Anything bad that ever befell me is advertised as punishment for my sins."

His expression hardened with her every word, until his face seemed to be hewn from granite. "Everything you just mentioned, everything you achieved and are, makes you only enterprising and powerful, a role model all women in and out of your region should aspire to emulate."

She let loose an incredulous laugh. At his imperiously

questioning look she explained, "It's just funny to hear you say what my baby sisters always do. But *they* are incapable of being impartial when it comes to me."

"I'm totally partial when it comes to you. I also happen to be absolutely right."

She again barely stopped herself from doing something impulsive. That was, more so than coming up to this suite. Something like throwing herself against his massive chest and smothering him in kisses. Which she might end up doing soon. Exposure to him was chipping away at any control she had left.

Watching her with that intensity that compromised her will, he said, "Your sisters are astute young ladies for making you their role model. You're the perfect one."

She waved his words away. "Let's not exaggerate, okay? I'd just die if they followed in some of my footsteps."

"Why? You're not proud of your achievements?"

"Those I'm proud of. I'm not proud of my mistakes."

"What are those? A failed, short-lived marriage? You think that disqualifies you as an inspiration?"

"Catastrophic choices certainly do. In my bid for freedom and independence, I made more than one. Like marrying the first man who seemed to be the opposite of the chauvinistic men I was used to, and finding out very soon he had equally objectionable traits, only on the other side of the spectrum. But whether I deserved it or not, I *was* their role model, and I strove to fill my position. The one thing I mourned most about being forced to marry Hassan was that I could no longer be that to them."

"You'll always be what your sisters look up to." He loomed over her as he sat up, his gaze seething with something she could only think was affront on her behalf. "Now tell me exactly how Hassan is forcing you into marriage. Leave out nothing."

Taking a huge breath, she started explaining everything.

He listened, his focus on her so total, it made it hard to speak. But she did, and she left nothing out as he'd demanded.

His expression grew almost scary as he listened, but he remained silent even after she finished, until she started to vibrate with tension. What if, now that he knew the extent of Zafrana's debts, he realized he couldn't do anything for her and apologized for giving her false hope?

Then he finally spoke, his voice a blade. "I knew about the debts, but I didn't know they were that crippling, or that the internal situation in Zafrana was that volatile."

"Father wouldn't have thought of asking me to do this for anything less."

He raised his hand, his jaw muscles bunching. "Nothing is worth imposing on you in any way, let alone sacrificing you. He should have sacrificed himself."

"He would have if it would have solved the problem."

"He should have considered any measures but bartering you to that old goat."

She burst out laughing. At his grim frown, she spluttered, "That's exactly what I called him earlier this evening to Zeena." At the growing thundercloud that gripped his face, she sobered. "What would you have done?"

"You don't want to know."

She gasped, for those five words painted a clear picture. This man was as deadly as she'd thought earlier, and not figuratively. He was no stranger to eliminating enemies. Even with his own hands.

Before she could process what kind of disaster she might have instigated by seeking his intervention, he demanded, "I need the specifics of those debts."

She latched on to the relatively innocuous subject. "Of course. You need to know everything before deciding whether you can help, or even if you'd want to."

He shot her one of those authoritatively reprimanding

glances. "Those specifics have no bearing on my decision. That was final since the moment I gave you my word. They are only for devising the most effective attack."

She shot up straight. "Attack?"

His eyes became icy emeralds. "There will be extreme measures employed in releasing Zafrana from Saraya's shackles."

Her heart hammered in dismay. "Define *extreme*."

"Eliminating the problem at the source."

"And how would you do that?"

"That's my business."

"Actually, it's mine, too. Mine, mainly. I'm the one who asked for this, and if you're going to do anything to...to hurt Hassan, I'd have to withdraw my request."

"You care what happens to him?"

"No, but I don't want him to meet with an unnatural end, either. For Saraya. For Najeeb. For peace's sake."

She thought his eyes flared at Najeeb's mention, but he only said, "Peace is always achieved after a war. A war always comes with heavy losses."

"I don't want freedom that comes at such a price."

"You think I'd kill him, don't you?"

"You sure made it sound like that."

"His demise *can* be easily arranged." As she started to splutter in alarm, his lips twisted in a lethal smile. "But it just happens I'm not considering liquidating him. Just his chokehold over Zafrana, and with it, most of his assets."

She held his gaze until she decided he was telling the truth, then collapsed back in relief. "For a moment there I thought I'd just signed Hassan's death warrant."

"It *is* the preferable, cleaner solution." As her heart pounded again, he added, "But I won't let him off that easy. Hassan's actions deserve protracted punishment before I even consider granting him reprieve."

"You still make it sound as if you'll end up offing him!"

When he only shrugged, she sat up again and threw her hands up in the air. "*Ya Ullah*...I can't believe we're sitting here haggling over the pros and cons of assassinating Hassan."

"To off him or not to off him, that is the question."

That, and his bedeviling expression, made her burst out laughing. "You fiend! You had me going there." Melting back again, she grinned. "So what do you intend to do, for real?"

"Which part of *that's my business* don't you get? You made the demand, now sit back while I take care of it as I see fit."

"Beggars can't be choosers, huh?"

"You'd never be anything but what you are, a princess whose demands must always be met."

His over-the-top statements kept leaving her breathless, her lips tingling with the need to taste them at the origin.

But she still had to make sure of one thing. "If my requests are that important to you, promise you won't go overboard. Just do enough to set me free, and hopefully set Zafrana back on the road to economic independence. I don't want any fallout to hit my father or Zafrana. Or Saraya."

He inclined his magnificent head, making her again wish he'd release his raven's-wing silk from its imprisoning band. "I promise I will be surgical. My excisions will leave the whole region healthier. Just for you."

Breath left her on a choppy exhalation. "You're really going to do this." She shook her head dazedly. "Wow... just give me a second to get my head around all of this."

"Take all the time you need." He did this heart-melting gesture again, reaching for a lock of her hair and rubbing it in utmost enjoyment between his fingers. "But you can start celebrating your restored freedom right now."

Moved to the brink of tears, she squeezed her eyes shut.

When she finally opened them, they'd filled her eyes, soaked her voice. "I need to apologize."

He frowned. "Never apologize, not to me. But what do you think you should apologize for?"

"For what I thought when I first thought of asking you for this."

"What did you think?"

"That you'd never do anything out of the goodness of your heart. That you don't have one."

A mirthless huff escaped him. "You were right. I don't have one. Not in any humanly accepted sense."

"From where I'm sitting, you have something better. I thought you'd never do anything for anyone without something of equal or more value in it for you, and I was wrong."

"Maybe you should withdraw your apology. Since you weren't wrong. I do want something."

Her heart forgot to beat. "You do?"

"Yes." He held her gaze in the snare of his. "An heir."

Three

"An heir."

Jen heard her voice as if coming from someone else. Reaching her ears from the end of a vortex of incomprehension.

The hypnosis in Numair's gaze only intensified, as if he was compelling her to say what he wanted her to say.

Good luck with that. It was a miracle she'd been able to produce sound at all, to parrot him. After the agitated excitement of meeting him, the soaring hope that he'd restore her freedom, the release of all tension when she'd made sure he would, it hadn't shocked her when he'd said that he had a price. What had flabbergasted her was the price itself. She couldn't even process it.

He couldn't have *really* said… "An heir?"

At her croaking question, without any change in his expression, he inclined his head. "Yes. An heir you'll give me."

Ya Ullah, he'd said it again. And this time he left no doubt who would provide him with said heir.

The expansive room started spinning, and the sick sensations that earlier had her in their grip crashed back on her. She pressed her head into the headrest, as if to stop the churning. "You're not joking."

"I've never been more serious."

Feeling as if she'd fallen into a trap, nausea almost blinded her. "Why are you doing this?"

In response, he covered the space between them. Before she could think of scooting away, she found herself half draped over his great body, stunned by his sheer strength.

"Doing what?" His whisper fanned her face, and the fragrant, virile scent of his breath and flesh only made the room spin harder. She tried to fidget out of his embrace, but he had her head cradled in the nook of his arm, supported by his muscle-laden shoulder, and her face tilted to look up at him. "Being truthful about what I want? I thought you appreciated total honesty."

"When did you decide you wanted it?" she whispered. "You can't have come up with it when I asked you to help me." She tried to shake her head and only felt the world spin again. He secured her tighter and her queasiness quieted. She moaned, in relief this time. "I thought you would have a price, but I never thought it could be something like that."

"What did you think it would be? Yourself?"

Now that he'd said it out loud, it felt presumptuous for the idea to have crossed her mind. But given his apparent interest in her, it had been the only thing she could think of.

She'd thought the most he'd want would be a short affair, maybe only while he passed through New York this time. But she wouldn't have considered that a price. It would have been a reward to be with the first and only man she'd wanted breathlessly on sight. In any other circumstances, she would have given anything to be with him, no matter how fleetingly. To have both him and her freedom would have been the most incredible opportunity of her life.

But it was clear she'd read the situation all wrong. No, she couldn't read it at all.

This was totally incomprehensible.

A gentle finger below her chin tilted her face up to him, his brooding gaze capturing her wandering eyes. "I never bargain for sexual favors, and I certainly would never take advantage of a woman's need in any other way."

Now that he put it that way, she again felt silly for thinking what she had. This was a man who must have his pick of the rare beauties and celebrities of the world, and there was no way he'd ever paid for his pleasures. She couldn't see a woman alive who wouldn't react to him like she had, wouldn't want him at any cost.

He went on. "I also never stomached passing liaisons, but I never had any desire for anything more. My life revolved around work and amassing wealth and power. Those were everything I wanted for as long as I can remember. Then recently, everything changed."

Curiosity, and something poignant and more powerful— empathy—dragged her out of her confused dismay.

Had he suffered some recent life-changing crisis that made him take stock of his life, forced him to reassess his lifestyle?

She realized he was waiting for her to ask before he elaborated. So she forced her constricted throat to release the question. "What happened?"

"I hit forty, and it made me feel I need to rearrange my priorities and adjust my path. It never bothered me before that I have no family, and no one to leave my fortune and legacy to. Now it does."

She gaped at him. This was again the last thing she'd expected he'd say. She'd expected a reason as unique and earth-shattering as he was. He was the last person on earth she would have believed could have a midlife crisis.

Maybe she'd read him wrong all along. Just like she'd been way off the mark in assessing what he'd want in return for helping her. But she still could think of no reason that he'd want an heir from her, of all women.

She put her bewilderment into words. "So you decided to join the human race after a lifetime of just dominating it. But now you feel the urge to perpetuate your genes. If you make your desire known, women would form lines spanning the globe for a chance to be the one to give you your heir."

"I *am* making my desire known. To the only woman I ever considered for the role."

Her confusion deepened. "Why would you consider me at all, let alone have me on a short list of one?"

"To borrow your earlier words, you're kidding, right?"

"To borrow yours, I've never been more serious."

He caught her chin between those powerful, roughened fingers. "How can you be? You're here with me—" he gathered her tighter against his incredible heat and hardness, making her senses whirl harder, her every muscle liquefy even more "—in my arms, within an hour of meeting. You would have been there within minutes had we been in different circumstances. The attraction between us combusted the moment I stepped into that ballroom, and it's been raging higher ever since."

She still couldn't believe she affected him as intensely as he did her. Even if she did, that wasn't an acceptable explanation. "I can understand this would make you want me in your bed—"

He interrupted her. "And you would have considered that a fair price in return for my services?"

"Your *services* would have been circumstantial, since

I would have come to your bed anyway, if you wanted me there."

At her admission, his eyes simmered with a triumphant glow. Which was weird, really. Didn't he already know any woman would throw herself at his feet, if only he would let her?

But it was clear her words didn't only please him, they stoked his lust. The heat emanating from him rose, igniting her own higher, and the hardness below her became a steel shaft of discomfort digging into her thigh. Her core throbbed with an empty ache she'd only ever felt since he'd touched her.

She wanted to wind herself around him, to tell him to forget everything—her need for his *services* and his for an heir—and act on the need burning them up.

Instead, she said, "As I was saying, even if you wanted me on sight, that still doesn't translate to considering me for the role of mother of your heir. From my vast experience with the obscenely rich and powerful, sexual desire is not even among the prerequisites in choosing who to procreate with. I'm sure a man like you has strict criteria for said role, and countless other women who're better candidates for it than me."

"I may be obscenely rich and powerful, but I already told you I care nothing about anyone's rules. I make and follow my own." Sensual appreciation weighed down his lids, filled his lips as his hand painted her from shoulders to buttocks in luxurious caresses. "But I do have extremely strict criteria in the mother of my heir. That's why only you will do."

"Why? Do I somehow fulfill more criteria than others?"

"You fulfill every single one, and others I didn't even have till I met you." He cupped her cheek hungrily, his gaze devouring her. "I want my heir to be born of the perfect woman."

This made her snort. "Boy, are you barking up the wrong woman. I'm so far from perfect I'm in another galaxy."

His fingers sank into her hair, gave a pleasurable tug at her nape. "You are perfect to me. Just like I, with all of my glaring flaws, am perfect to you."

Her snort was more indelicate this time. "What glaring flaws? You *are* perfect, and would be so in anyone's eyes."

"Would I? That's news to me, since both allies and foes consider me a monster." Before she could object, he pressed on. "From what you know of the business world, you must know what it took to rise to my current status and to maintain it. You know I must be ruthless and remorseless, and that I don't give a damn what the world thinks of me, and that nothing is beyond me. From our interactions so far, you must realize I'm dangerous, even deadly, and I can destroy anyone I decide deserves it, even kill them, without turning a hair."

She stared at him. He'd put everything she'd felt about him in her bones into words. Everything that made him even more perfect to her.

She nodded slowly. "Instinctively, and logically, I know you're all that."

His lips spread in satisfaction. "All that makes me the opposite of perfect to everyone. Except for my partners, I'm someone to dread, or at most to appease, either in the hope of winning my favor or avoiding my danger. As for the women who pursue me, most risk it for the lure of said obscene power and wealth, and a few for the misguided fantasy of attempting to tame the most dangerous predator there is. But all fear me, and none trust me." His arms squeezed her tighter into his containment, his eyes growing more possessive. "You're the only one to ever see me for what I am, scales and claws and fangs and all, and instead of putting you off, everything about me is exactly what appeals to you. As you say in your region, I'm the one to *yemla ainek*—the one to 'fill your eye.'"

It was as if he was reading her mind. More, her deepest, most private beliefs and yearnings.

Again she nodded, not even thinking of contesting his verdict. "I left naiveté and idealism behind when I was seven, grew up in the cutthroat worlds of highest-level politics and business. I've long since learned that the best men need to have a lot of monster in them to be merciless enough to make the painful decisions, cunning enough to beat evil at its game, strong enough to enforce harsh changes for the better and resilient enough to be the one left standing after a war and doing as much good as possible in this crazy world."

His eyes darkened with her every word, until those fathomless black pupils engulfed the glowing emerald. She felt as if she was watching a panther in the seconds before he pounced. And she couldn't wait for him to. Even when she knew she might not survive his ferocity.

Then he did. Growling deep in his gut like his namesake, he brought her fully over him, making her feel she was no more than a twenty-pound baby. It should have been terrifying to realize just how much stronger than her he was. But his roughness was infused with such care, it only sent all her senses soaring.

She tumbled over him, the skirt of her dress riding up as he splayed her thighs wide, had her straddling him. The moment she felt him fully against her, between her legs, she almost fainted with the spike of arousal. Then his lips opened over her neck, and she did swoon. Her head fell back, giving him fuller access, surrendering to his pleasuring.

She needed this, needed him, come what may.

"You feel and taste even better than I imagined. Jenan..."

She jerked as if at the sting of a lash when he said her

name. She'd never liked her full name. Now it inflamed her to hear it on his lips, in that voracious growl. But he was sending her out of her mind with everything he did. The way he moved against her, breathed her in, touched and kneaded and suckled her… It was all too much.

And too little. She needed more. Everything. His mouth and hands all over her, his potency inside her.

"Numair…"

At hearing her moaning his name, the same desperation she felt reverberating inside her seemed to emanate from his body in shock waves. Then he swept her around and brought her under him on the couch, then bore down on her.

The world disappeared again, nothing remaining in her awareness but his greed and urgency and lust dominating her.

Spreading her thighs around his hips, he pressed between them, his hardness grinding against her entrance through their clothes. Her back arched deeply to accommodate him, a cry tearing from her very recesses at the feel of him, the sight of him above her.

"Jenan." His growl sounded pained as he surveyed her for one last second. Then his lips claimed hers, branding them. She opened wide to his invasion, and his tongue thrust deep, singeing her with pleasure, breaching her with need, draining her of reason.

Pressure built—behind her eyes, inside her chest, deep in her loins. Her hands convulsed on his arms, digging into his muscles, everything inside her surging, gushing, needing anything and everything he'd do to her. His fingers and tongue and teeth exploiting her every secret, his manhood filling that distressing void he'd created inside her…

Something buzzed against her thigh, made her lurch beneath him. After moments it stopped. Then it started again until it finally made him stiffen above her. Then he was cursing viciously as he rose off her.

The moment she lost his anchoring, she whimpered. His tempestuous glance told her he was feeling exactly the same. Wild with hunger and frustration.

He whipped out his phone in barely controlled fury. He only bit off a few phrases before ending the call. She vaguely understood it was one of his Black Castle partners. It figured only one of them would warrant Numair interrupting their first kiss.

As she finished the thought, she found herself snickering. First kiss indeed. First ravishing more like.

Numair's grimace filled with mock reproach and a too-real self-deprecation as he surveyed her still boneless condition. "I'm glad one of us is not in agony, and can still laugh."

"I'm not laughing... I'm snickering."

His huff sounded genuinely amused, not to mention surprised. "Thanks for the correction. Care to share the source of your merriment? I can use something to take my mind off the urge to hunt Antonio down for interrupting us. Or to pounce back on you and finish what I started."

Before she blurted out for him to just do the latter, she remembered they'd been in the middle of a game-changing conversation. And they hadn't reached a resolution yet. There might not be even one to reach.

Dismay finally made her pull herself up from her flagrant surrender. Numair remained towering over her as she sat up, like some all-powerful genie from a fable. The searing sensuality of his scowl made it almost impossible for her not to pull him back over her. Only the "heir" thing stopped her.

Before she could reintroduce the subject, Numair suddenly came down beside her again and, with shocking ease, pulled her back onto his lap.

After sealing her gasping lips in a kiss that robbed her of volition, he pulled back, his eyes smoldering, explicit with what he'd do to her once she stopped arguing.

"Do you still have any questions why I chose you?" He took a hand to his lips, nibbled on it in lieu of her mouth and had her gasping and squirming in pleasure. "It's because I don't want my heir to only be born of the perfect woman, but of perfect pleasure. And it is perfection between us. The way we make each other feel is magical. And I will accept nothing less. I will have nothing else."

She had no more arguments about that. It was magic. At least for her. But if he said it was the same for him, she had to believe him. He had no reason to lie or even exaggerate.

Almost all men in her experience had reason to do both. They thought all desert kingdoms swam in oil money, didn't believe her when she'd said Zafrana didn't. Even those who did believe her still thought she was talking relative poverty in the millions instead of billions. She'd had too many imposters try to land the loaded princess they'd thought she was. Her ex had been one of those.

But Numair was far richer and more powerful than her whole kingdom put together, with Saraya thrown in for good measure. She could only believe what he said, and that the desire he displayed was 100 percent real.

But he'd spoiled it all with that heir talk.

He was now suckling her fingers, each pull a stab of pleasure in her core. It was almost painful to stop him, to relinquish the delight, but she had to make him realize how preposterous she found his demand.

"Numair…I do want you, completely, even mindlessly." He growled and pressed her harder into his erection, dragging another moan from her depths. "But no matter how much I want you, I can't act on my desire when I know your sole purpose of sleeping with me is so I'd give you a baby."

He gave the finger he'd been suckling a sharp nip, heightening her distress. "It's far from my sole purpose. It's actually the product of my *only* purpose now. Untold pleasure. Which I will give, and take, as often as you can stand."

She squirmed over his lap, making both their conditions worse. "What if it turned out to be a disappointment instead? What if all those initial fireworks fizzled out, and we turned out to be incompatible in bed?"

His lip curl was dismissal itself. "We will be incendiary. The moment you say yes, I'll demonstrate."

Feeling squeezed into a tighter corner as his every word decimated her arguments, she still asked, "When you say heir, you mean a male child, right? What if I agree to your insane proposition, and I get pregnant with a girl? Or I can't get pregnant? Or you can't father children?"

His smile became more forbearing, as if he considered her what-ifs ridiculous, and her adorable as she worked herself up in a lather.

"Finished enumerating your worst-case scenarios?" He shrugged a shoulder, making everything she'd said irrelevant. "You only have to say yes and I'll take care of the rest."

She had to laugh. "I did think you were a god when I laid eyes on you, but you clearly think you are literally one, if you think you can make fate bow to your desires like that."

He gave another nonchalant shrug. "I always create my fate to my specifications. As I'm doing right now. I recognized you as the one tailored to my every need and demand. Once I have you, I'll fulfill every major milestone I have left in my life's master plan."

That made her sit up on his lap. "Okay, time out. I know you're master of all you survey and all, but even you must know how crazy you just sounded. I hate to break it to you, but there is stuff in life that is outside your control."

"We can and do control our destinies. You can either relinquish control over yours by considering others who'd never truly appreciate your sacrifice or even fully benefit from it, or you can say yes to me and take control of your fate."

"How would being an instrument in *your* so-called master plan make me mistress of my own fate?"

"Because contrary to everyone else in your life, I will never threaten your autonomy. At your demand, I will only boost your powers, support your plans and remove obstacles from your path. You will *choose* to say yes to me, because you'll weigh all pros and cons, and the pros will crash heavily in my favor. Once you do, we'll become lovers. I'll give you anything you've ever wished for, in and out of bed."

"When you say pros and cons, getting rid of Hassan is among the pros, right? You *are* making this quid pro quo."

"No. I promised I'd rid you and Zafrana of Hassan, and I will, no matter what happens between us. You can immediately tell your father you've found a solution for all your problems and are sending Hassan to hell." He nibbled the fleshy side of her hand, and she involuntarily pressed harder into him in response. "You will become my lover and bear my heir because of a dozen other reasons, all borne of your free will. The foremost one is because you can't wait to be in my bed, taken and mastered, serviced and pleasured."

He punctuated his last words with suckles and nips that had every cell in her body clamoring for everything he'd just tantalized her with.

"What free will?" she moaned, deep and long. "*Ya Ullah*, Numair, now I know what it feels like to be swept along on a deluge. You *are* one."

"I will sweep you into a realm neither of us has ever entered, one of pure pleasure. Then when you become pregnant, we'll marry."

She choked. She coughed until she felt as if her life force would be expelled. As Numair realized her distress, his efforts to end her paroxysm only made things worse.

When the shock-induced attack finally came to an end, she looked up at him through eyes that felt inflamed. "Why can't you be like other men and just do the obvious thing? I ask you for a huge favor, and you ask for one in return and be done with it? You had to go demand an heir, and now marriage? Who said marriage was an option at all?"

His face became implacable. "I do. And it wouldn't be an option. It would be a must."

This made her push out of his arms, needing to put some breathable space between them. "Thanks, but no thanks. I was married once, and it isn't for me. The most I fantasized about was a hot affair with a sex god who had the power to get my kingdom out of its worst historical bind. I'm not up for becoming a wife. Certainly not to a man who, when all is said and done, considers me the best specimen to procreate with."

His lips pursed disapprovingly as he watched her scooting away from him. "Apart from the blatant inaccuracy of this last statement, you've already discussed having a child with me, which means you were considering it. What did you expect you would do once you were carrying my child? That you'd have it in secret, give it to me and disappear? Or that you'd have it out of wedlock, a princess from your region of all places? Or did you think you'd have it here and cut all ties with your kingdom? And where did you figure I'd be in all this? On the sidelines, content to see my child once every blue moon? Sending checks and not taking any role in its upbringing?" Before she could think of a response to his barrage, he declared, "We *will* get married as soon as you become pregnant."

Bombarded by his inexorable will, she felt as if she'd choke again. Before she succumbed once more, she fumbled for the purse she'd dropped on the coffee table, then stood up unsteadily.

Once she'd taken a few air-filled steps away from him, she said, "I need time to think."

Then, on trembling legs, she strode out. He let her walk away.

As she opened the main door of the suite, she almost crumpled to the ground with fright when he caught her back.

She could *swear* she'd walked here all alone!

As he turned her, she started spluttering, "How…?"

He drowned her in a kiss that ended any possibility for independent thought or movement.

It was him who finally released her, only the storms in his eyes betraying his state of emotional and physical arousal.

Before he let her spill out the door, he said, "I'm giving you till tomorrow evening, then I will send my right hand for you. Tomorrow night, you sleep in my arms."

Four

Numair watched Jenan receding down the corridor as if she was escaping a widening chasm.

Every step taking her away from him had him vibrating with dread that he'd just committed the biggest mistakes of his life. Letting her go, and before that, introducing the subject of heir and marriage so prematurely.

What if, in spite of the unstoppable desire that had exploded into existence between them, he'd come on too strong, and she'd run away thinking it the better fate to marry Hassan, a man she'd find far easier to handle?

Expending the last of what he'd previously thought was limitless willpower, he squashed the urge to stalk her, haul her back inside, lock every door and simply overpower her reluctance and misgivings. He might have decreed he'd take her tomorrow night, but everything in him was roaring for him to claim her right now.

But he'd already cornered himself, making it impossible

to do anything but watch her go. Anything he did now to override her would only make things worse.

He didn't recognize himself in this condition, as he'd never been almost out of control. He'd never been unable to project the consequences of his actions, had never acted on impulse or taken a step without premeditation. His brothers had always said he was the epitome of what it meant to be Machiavellian.

But everything he'd done since he'd seen Jenan hadn't even been actions but reactions, all unpremeditated and uncalculated. He was suffering from something he'd never experienced. A form of insanity.

And it was because of her. Jenan. He was beginning to think she was truly her name. At least one meaning of it.

The meaning he was sure her parents had meant was the plural of *jennah*—garden, what the ancients called paradise. That meaning was apt, too. But it was the colloquial meaning of the word that was relevant to his condition, what he now suspected she could induce. Madness.

But even in his state, he wasn't so far gone he didn't realize she was returning to her Tribeca apartment in lower Manhattan alone. Whether by cab or her own car, it was still a fifteen-minute drive and it was now—he flicked a glance at his watch—2:00 a.m. Time had really flown with her.

But it would compound his self-sabotaging behavior to follow her now. To ensure her safety without further damages, he would have to settle for having her followed.

The moment she disappeared around the corner, he whipped out his phone, called Ameen, sent him a photo of her from the digital file he had on her, ordered him to tail her home then report to him.

Afterward, he stared at the photo. It superficially resembled the woman he'd spent the past six hours with. It was like a lookalike, the mask she presented to the world, hiding her true nature. The charisma that leaped in her eyes, the wit and whimsy that played on her lips and the sheer impact she'd had on his senses in reality were absent. Even so, heat spread inside him just looking at the photo, when before meeting her, he'd surveyed it with the utmost clinical coldness.

Finally closing the door, he went back inside, homing in on the spot where he'd almost made love to her.

Sitting down, he caressed the place where she'd sat, feeling her warmth, even when there was no way it was still detectable. But then her feel was imprinted on his hands, permeating his senses. Her breath still filled his lungs, and her taste still tingled on his tongue.

Jenan. Mind-twisting, will-warping madness.

He'd wanted to possess her every second of the hours he'd spent with her. But he'd managed to hold back, to do what he'd thought more vital—negotiate the terms of future, limitless intimacies. Then she'd revealed her convictions, so serious and unwavering as she lay soft and surrendering in his embrace. She'd exposed the indomitable realist who'd smashed cultural and gender restraints, who didn't have a smidge of silliness or squeamishness in her expectations, who'd taken on the world and won.

Everything she was explained why she'd hit him that hard. The infallible instincts that had steered him throughout a nightmarish existence, had made him not only survive but triumph over everything and everyone, had recognized her. She had been made to understand him, to withstand him, to appreciate the monster inside him when it sent everyone else cowering.

Rationing his response had ceased to be an option.

He would have taken her, and she would have let him if not for the interruption. Now frustration ate through him. Not that having her would have quenched this blazing need. It would have only left him hungrier for her. He'd never known such ferocious desire existed, or that he of all people could be victim to it. But everything with her had been the most exhilarating thing that had ever happened to him. The attraction that had arced between them had been the most invigorating thing he'd ever experienced.

It was also the most dangerous.

It had messed up his fine-tuned conquering methods, pulverized his impregnable rules. It had reduced him to a reactive, starving man who didn't follow plans and didn't have brakes. He'd never once considered the possibility that he wouldn't get everything he wanted. He'd always gotten his every planned result because he'd never cared what anyone thought of him. People had always been most welcome to hate or despise him as long as they bowed to him. How they bowed had never been a concern. In fact, he'd always preferred to force them to their knees.

But he couldn't afford—no, couldn't *contemplate*— that Jenan would feel any aversion, or even reluctance toward him. He had to have her early eagerness back. He had to have that total trust and admiration lighting up her face again.

He had to have *her*.

And to think he'd come tonight bent on systematically seducing Khalil Aal Ghamdi's daughter to obtain his vital heir. But what he'd planned in cold blood had turned into a consuming need. Now instead of gritting his teeth and mating with a woman he'd been certain wouldn't arouse his most basic urge, he would burn in the raging flames of his desire for Jenan. If their brief time of delirium was anything to go by, he was in for the untold pleasure he'd promised her. More. He was in for the first true pleasure of his life.

If only Antonio hadn't called when he had. He would have been inside her now, taking her to the first peak of many. But it was a paramount rule of the Black Castle brotherhood, a rule *he'd* made, to immediately respond to any communication from a brother. With their lethal pasts and perilous presents, no one knew when it might be a matter of life or death.

But Antonio hadn't been in danger. For some reason he didn't give a damn about, he'd picked then of all times to recommend a few more hypnotherapy sessions for Numair.

Cursing vehemently, he reached for his phone, then paused. Though Antonio had called him barely half an hour ago, he could now be asleep.

Once their brotherhood's field surgeon in their years as the slaves of The Organization, Antonio had become Black Castle Enterprise's resident medical genius, the creator and director of their avant-garde and booming medical R&D business, and a surgeon who was one of the world's most brilliant and unorthodox. He kept hours as extreme and unpredictable as everything about him. He was also known to sleep at will, to charge his batteries whenever possible for the grueling days he maintained in his lab, the OR and the boardroom. Numair had seen him fall asleep sitting up, in under thirty seconds. It was very possible he'd fallen asleep immediately after his fateful phone call.

But so what? He hoped Antonio was in deep, blissful sleep after months of severe deprivation, or on the verge of orgasm with a woman he'd been panting after for years. He'd love to return the favor.

He almost drove his finger through Antonio's speed-dial number. By the third ring, Numair was ready to storm out, raid Antonio's Fifth Avenue penthouse and punch him awake.

Then the line clicked open, and Antonio's calmly teasing voice came on. "I thought you wanted to kill me when I called earlier."

"I did," Numair bit off. "I still do."

"I interrupted something major, huh?"

"You interrupted *the* major something. And you weren't even dying."

"So this is a courtesy call for our history's sake, before you come make sure I rectify my oversight?"

Any man would have been worried if he'd inadvertently cost Numair what Antonio had tonight. But having faced death on an almost daily basis together, and defended each other with their lives for over fifteen years, Antonio had reason not to fear Numair's retaliation. Not that he feared anything. Antonio was the most imperturbable being who'd ever lived. Even more than any of them. Numair wouldn't be surprised if his nerves were made of actual steel.

He finally asked, "Why the hell did you call, Bones?"

"I told you why, Phantom."

They always reverted to those code names, what they'd known each other by in The Organization. Those who remembered their names had been forbidden to use them. Numair hadn't remembered his, Phantom being the one name he'd known most of his life.

He'd been among hundreds of boys who'd been plucked from all over the world and taken to that isolated installation in the Balkans and turned into mercenaries. He'd been too young when he'd been taken but had still been "broken in," punished if he mentioned anything from his previous life. He'd first been conditioned to respond to a number. The name Phantom had come much later. He'd forgotten everything about his past. All that had remained of his memories before he'd come to what he'd later called Black Castle had been the name of his panther toy, Numair, and what he'd much later realized were the names of desert kingdoms, Saraya and Zafrana. And the memory of drowning.

He'd spent over twenty-five years of his forty in Black Castle before he'd orchestrated his and his brothers' escape ten years ago. He'd spent most of those in frustration, unable to build an investigation into his origins on the sparse memories he had. Not knowing who he was had remained a gaping hole in his being.

Then Antonio had finally developed a method of aggressive hypnosis tailored to Numair's condition and character. He'd thought it would be effective, but warned it could be dangerous. But Numair would have risked anything to find out the truth. He'd been certain someone had been responsible for his decades-long ordeal, and he wouldn't rest until he'd found them and made them pay.

Antonio's efforts had seemed to be another dead end, but he'd already expected that initial failure, since Numair was resistant to hypnosis. He'd never expected it to be anything but a long-term therapy as they'd been excavating memories Numair had before he'd been four.

But long-term was what Numair was all about. He'd started planning his escape from The Organization when he hadn't even been ten. He'd put it into action twenty years later.

In captivity, Numair had grown up fast, toughening into steel and developing an undetectable cunning that had enabled him to navigate his ruthless environment and manipulate his monstrous jailors. By ten he'd already carved a place for himself as the establishment's most valuable acquisition and future asset. Based on his uncanny abilities in every skill it took to make the best spy, they'd changed his name from a four-digit number to Phantom, beginning a trend of calling boys by names that symbolized them.

But he'd known he wouldn't be able to escape alone. He had to have help. And in turn, help others escape. Recognizing six boys, all younger than himself, as kindred spirits who had superior abilities complementing his own, he'd manipulated their captors into making them his team. He'd made each swear a blood oath to live for their broth-

erhood and for one goal—to one day escape and destroy
The Organization, saving other children from their fate.

They had implemented his convoluted plan, and after
they'd escaped, they'd built new identities and created
Black Castle Enterprises, using their unique skills. That
was, all but Cypher. He'd left their brotherhood after an
explosive falling out. He'd pledged they'd never see him
again. They hadn't.

Though Cypher's loss remained an open wound in their
brotherhood, they'd compensated by focusing on their original pact, dismantling The Organization from the outside
in, methodically and undetectably.

Meanwhile, each also pursued his personal quest, for
the family he'd been taken from, the heritage he'd been
stripped of or for a new purpose and direction. Their bigger quest was sometimes forced to the background until
more pressing personal issues were resolved, as it had during Rafael's quest for vengeance and Raiden's quest to reclaim his heritage. Both men had achieved their purposes,
and unexpectedly found wives, too. Now it was his turn.

Four months ago, Antonio's hypnosis had borne fruit,
and he'd remembered enough to finally piece together his
history. He'd found out how he'd ended up in The Organization's grasp. And who he really was.

So what had the damned Antonio been thinking when
he'd called earlier?

He again flayed Antonio with his exasperation. "Why
in hell did you suddenly think I need more sessions? Their
objective has already been achieved."

Antonio switched to doctor mode, this frustrating, all-
knowing attitude. "That's what you decided, not me. Your
memories were so deeply buried and so partially formed
in the first place, then so fractured by trauma and suppres-
sion, I was forced to pull back constantly. I had to spread

out the sessions, dig over a longer period or risk damaging your psyche and sanity."

That was news to Numair. "You mean you could have forced memories to the surface faster? You took all those years intentionally?"

"Didn't you hear the part where I said *or risk damaging your psyche and sanity*?"

"You actually think I have anything inside my head that could be damaged?"

"As my mentor and slave driver, I would have said your head is made of solid steel. But as your doctor, I've touched a few deeply hidden and relatively softer spots. The consistency of rock, granted, but under enough pressure even steel can snap and rock can be pulverized."

"Where is this leading exactly?"

"You remember—no pun intended—the key memory that was the basis of your investigations into your origins?"

He remembered nothing more. Once the memory had exploded in his mind, he'd felt as if he'd been reliving it. It had been so real he'd almost drowned before Antonio had pulled him out of the hypnotic state.

That memory was of him on a yacht with his father when men, who looked like monsters in his memories, had boarded them. His father had been struck unconscious then thrown overboard. Numair had no doubt he'd drowned immediately. Then the men had tossed him after his father.

He should have drowned, too. And he'd always remembered the sensations of drowning, what had spawned an unreasoning hatred of swimming, even as he'd been forced to excel in it. More probing had unearthed memories of swimming lessons since he'd been born. Investigations had revealed he'd managed to swim to shore in Turkey, where he'd been taken to an orphanage. Over a year later, an Organization recruiter had taken him. And his real ordeal had begun.

Analyzing the history of the whole region at the time, he'd found out that his father had been Hisham Aal Ghaanem, the then Crown Prince of Saraya. And he'd been his father's heir. He'd concluded that his father's assassination had been orchestrated by his brother, Saraya's current king, Hassan. Getting rid of him, too, had spared his uncle from being only regent until he came of age.

"I'd like to revisit that memory."

Antonio's demand ended his musings. "Why?"

"Humor me."

"No."

"Just no?"

"Yes, as long as you won't give me a reason beside wanting to strap me down and poke around in my head again."

"As if I want to poke around that dungeon you call a head. It's filled with rotting corpses and dismembered remains."

"As if your head isn't."

"It's my head, so I have to live with it. Infesting it with the contents of your far more nightmarish skull is up there in my priorities with contracting an incurable STD." Numair started to growl, and Antonio raised his voice, drowning his. "But I feel there are more fragments still stuck in there, like shrapnel. I'm worried if they surface on their own they'd cause uncharted damage. Before you scoff, just imagine yourself with the balance that keeps you precariously on the side of the angels shattered. With your power and intellect, you'd be a full-blown monster. So I'm really worried about the world here."

Numair hated to admit it, but in The Organization, he'd seen the kind of widespread mayhem caused by those who'd been irrevocably damaged by his kind of life—even when they were nowhere near his caliber.

He exhaled. "What memories could be more damaging than remembering my father's murder and my own near drowning?"

"I don't know. But I've been reviewing the videos and notes of our last sessions, and I'm convinced what you now know isn't the whole story."

"It's the relevant part of it."

"Why are you being so pigheaded? I thought you want to find everything about your past."

"I know enough."

It was Antonio's turn to exhale in exasperation. "As long as you understand you're ignoring my medical recommendation. And you run the risk of having those memories resurface and tear through whatever is keeping you from going berserk."

"I understand. Anything else?"

Antonio's huff was self-deprecating. "I should have implanted a posthypnotic suggestion in that impenetrable skull of yours when I had the chance."

"But you didn't." He infused his voice with the older brother's and leader's criticism his brothers had grown up with. "I always said your moral afflictions stop you from maximizing your opportunities."

"Yeah." Antonio sounded vexed, then he suddenly brightened. "But I can always hit you with a tranq dart and have my way with you."

"As if I wouldn't see you coming a mile away."

Antonio chuckled. "Go ahead, underestimate me. I'll have you on my table again yet, Phantom."

"Dream on, Bones."

Then as it was their way, with the conversation over, they just terminated the call with no lingering goodbyes.

Afterward, he sat there staring ahead, his conversation with Antonio forgotten, his mind again full of Jenan and how he'd come to meet her.

She was part of the other side of his heritage. His mother

was Safeyah Aal Ghamdi, a princess of the royal family in Zafrana, a cousin of the late king, Zayd Aal Ghamdi, and Jenan's distant relative. His mother had left the region after her husband and son had been presumed dead thirty-seven years ago and had never come back. She'd never re-married, and had died four years ago in England.

Then when Zafrana's king had died twenty-two years ago, the throne had gone to his closest male relative, his cousin Khalil, Jenan's father.

His plan coming here had been simple. To reclaim his heritage, and punish the monster who'd murdered his father and caused Numair to rot in hell for a quarter of a century.

He was still working on providing irrefutable proof of his identity. With his father being dead almost four decades, it was hard to find anything with his DNA. Proof positive was to find his remains, so he was scouring the Mediterranean where his father's yacht had sunk.

Once he found it, he'd reclaim his true identity. He didn't fear exposure, like Rafael Salazar, who'd been abducted from his parents. No one in The Organization knew who Numair really was, having obtained him as an anonymous child from an orphanage in a faraway country. And he'd make his story work perfectly with the meticulous history he'd created for his Numair Al Aswad persona.

Once he decided to announce his real identity, he'd reveal the part where he'd survived the assassination attempt. His story would diverge from the truth when he'd claim he'd been found by a fishing fleet on the shores of Damhoor, a neighboring kingdom to Saraya, and taken to an orphanage there. A couple who'd been working there had adopted him almost immediately, but had never announced it since adoption was forbidden there, taking him to the States as their biological son. They'd told him he was adopted only when he'd been in his late teens.

The other truth he'd say was that it had taken him all that time to investigate his origins.

Until he proved them, he planned to prepare the playing field. And to punish Hassan. Before he exposed him for the murderer he was and throw him in a dungeon for life, he'd first disgrace and destroy him a bit at a time. Everyone should be happy with that, since all monarchs in the region wished he'd abdicate the throne to one worthy of it. But that wouldn't be Hassan's crown prince and his cousin, the much-loved Najeeb, but Numair himself.

If his cousins contested his right to the throne, which he fully expected they would, he had the power to curb them and any allies whose help they enlisted, and the finances to buy them all a few times over. If not, he could escalate to whatever level of conflict it took to make them bow down to him. He had no problem taking the throne in a coup. Or starting a war to claim what was his. It wouldn't be the first time he'd instigated an armed conflict.

The other part of his plan had been to claim the other side of his heritage.

He'd come here bound on taking Zafrana's throne, too, and saving his other homeland from its inept king. The only way to do this was through blood. Khalil's blood. Through one of his daughters. Jenan had been the obvious choice, since her half sisters were so young. Then Hassan had made a bid for her, unintentionally trying to beat him to Zafrana with his same plan.

That had posed little change in his plan. Instead of claiming Jenan directly, he had to pulverize Hassan's bid first. He'd intended to seduce her, impregnate her then marry her, becoming Zafrana's de facto ruler during Khalil's life through the marriage alliance. After Khalil's death, when the throne became his child's, he'd intended to rule as regent until his child came of age.

Then in mere hours, everything had changed. His one

objective was now Jenan. Not because she was strategic to his plans, but because he had to have her.

Now he feared his marauding ways had alienated her.

He heaved up to his feet, his every muscle bunched as if in preparation for the fight of his life.

Not having her wasn't an option. He wouldn't retreat and change his approach. He'd escalate his attack, besiege her, leave her nowhere to run and hide.

Tomorrow night, Jenan *would* be his.

"You are my hero!"

Jen winced as Zeena launched herself at her the moment she opened the door for her and Fayza the next morning.

Fayza, her ball-of-energy nineteen-year-old sister, zipped around her and inside her apartment, excitement radiating from her eyes and spilling from her lips. "When they realized you disappeared from your own engagement party, Father and Hassan almost had strokes. Father with worry and Hassan with outrage. It was *so* funny."

Though her sisters were in such good cheer, she still worried. "Is Father okay?"

"Yeah." Fayza threw herself down on Jen's huge floral couch in the living room. "His blood pressure is just through the roof."

Jen groaned at what Fayza considered okay. "*Ya Ullah,* Fay, the way you take nothing seriously will one day give *me* a stroke! Please tell me you gave him his medication!"

"Yeah, yeah." Fayza rolled her hands, in a hurry to attack the next topic. "I bet it didn't work until we called him on the way up here to tell him you're okay."

But she wasn't okay, might never be okay again.

Since she'd left Numair, she'd been unable to sleep or even sit, pacing holes in her wall-to-wall carpeting, her stomach eating itself with tension and hunger, yet unable to tolerate even a sip of water. Every inch of her buzzed with excess electricity, every nerve so taut she felt they'd snap.

"You know, sis..." Fayza stretched out, her knee-length raven hair a sharp contrast to the pastel print sofa, her gold eyes glittering with mischief, her face the very sight of admiration and smugness. "We always thought you were a wonder woman, but that stunt you pulled last night? That qualifies you for an all-time record in sticking your tongue out to our collective region, culture and history." She guffawed, drummed her heels on the couch. "I would have given anything to see Hassan's face the moment he realized you'd just up and left." She jumped up onto her knees as Jen approached, draped herself over the couch's back like an inquisitive cat. "So what did you do instead of attending that funeral? Caught a movie? Went roller-skating? Or came back here, ordered pizza, watched Will and Grace reruns and did your toenails?"

"She left with a hunk from some Arabian Nights fable."

Zeena's enthusiastic declaration was followed by total silence as Fayza's irrepressible chatter came to an abrupt end. For three seconds. Then she exploded.

"*What?* And you didn't tell me? Zee, I'll kill you!"

Jen grimaced at her sister's loudness as Zeena sputtered, "Tell you what? All I know is that this genie seemed to appear out of nowhere, materialized beside Jen and then *poof*, they were both gone."

Jen had to laugh. As ridiculous as that account was, it sounded more plausible than what had actually happened.

Fayza turned excited eyes to Jen. "Spill!"

Knowing it was pointless to avoid their questions, Jen told them everything, with some key elements left out. Like Numair almost making love to her, and his pregnancy-to-marriage demand.

It was late in the day before Zeena and Fayza left, during which they did order pizza, watched Will and Grace reruns and did their nails—hands and feet.

The two girls floated away, buoyed by delight that their big sister wouldn't barter herself for their kingdom's peace and economic salvation, and that a knight in shining armor had charged to her rescue.

Jen closed the door behind them, slumped against it and let the smile she'd pinned on for their benefit crumble. If only they knew her knight was a black-as-sin marauder, and as unstoppable as a hurricane…

Though she still couldn't bring herself to do as he'd demanded—tell her father everything would be taken care of—she did believe Numair when he'd said she didn't have to say yes to his proposition in return for his help. That wasn't why she was in such turmoil.

It was his demand itself. Becoming his lover, sleeping in his arms, sharing every intimacy sounded deliriously fantastic. Since he'd touched her, she'd been aching with need for him. She felt certain he was the man who'd show her what sex could really be like, what passion and satisfaction were.

Yet getting pregnant by him? It sounded terrifying.

But what was her alternative? She could continue to live alone, work, succeed, exercise, volunteer… Rinse and repeat. Sure, that was great, and it had been good enough— before him. But she'd had the hope that she'd one day find a man and fall in love, at least in lust. But now she knew no other man would ever compare to Numair. She'd never look at another man twice, let alone share her body with him. So if she didn't indulge her feminine urges with Numair, she'd have to put them in deep freeze for life. That sounded as horrible as a lifelong prison sentence. Living in hope, even if it never came to pass, was one thing; knowing there was no hope was another.

As for having a baby, she'd always thought she'd one

day have one. But since she'd given up on marriage, and no one had tempted her to have sex with him, she'd thought she'd seek out a donor. But after Numair, that didn't feel like an option anymore. Now that she knew he existed, that she could want a man that much, that he wanted her as fiercely, how could she contemplate having a child not born of this *perfection*, as he'd said?

To have a child with this wonder *would* be incredible. And once she got pregnant, if they married as he'd insisted, he'd certainly never be a needy, clingy, exploitative partner, like her ex had been, so she had nothing to worry about in that arena. He'd also promised he'd never smother her. Realistically speaking, with a man like him, who was so preoccupied with burdens the magnitude of which she probably couldn't imagine, the opposite would probably be true. He'd probably have little time for her, giving her all the space she needed and then some.

His ardor would probably cool off gradually, too. And hers as well, no doubt, especially with a child changing the essence of her existence. Once things settled, she'd end up having everything she had now, plus a child and the best possible partner in raising it.

Though Numair felt as if he was missing human components, she had a feeling he would make a good father. That protector vibe told her he would. She knew in her bones she'd be safe with him, and so would a child.

In fact, the more she thought of it, the more it sounded too good to be true. She couldn't even imagine why all this was happening to her, of all women. It sounded like too much of a coincidence, too much the answer to her every fantasy. Everything about him, everything he'd said and done, was the best thing she could have hoped for. So was it what it appeared to be? Or was there somehow more to it?

She had a thousand questions. And worries. This man was the most unfathomable quantity she'd ever met. She knew there was *far* more to him than even she could imagine. And for some reason she couldn't even begin to explain, she felt there was far more to this whole thing…

The bell rang right at her back. She jumped as if at a close-range gunshot, blasted out of her reverie.

Her eyes tore to the clock on the wall. It was 7:00 p.m. This had to be Numair's right-hand man.

Heart hammering, she squared her shoulders. She *would* go to Numair. To ask him to have a long, rational talk.

She'd ask her questions, demand her terms—her safeguards, more like. Once he'd given her satisfactory answers and they had a roadmap of sorts, she'd tear his clothes off and demand he show her no mercy.

Inhaling a bolstering breath, she opened the door with the smile she'd patented for strangers. The next second her lungs almost burst in shock.

Numair. On her doorstep.

Before she could draw another breath, she was swept up as if she was made of cotton candy, in arms that defined power, looking up into a face that was mastery incarnate.

Kicking the door closed behind him, he looked down at her with a voracity that turned her body from solid to molten. And that was before his deep, devouring words hit her.

"I realized I've been remiss. I spoke of the untold pleasure I have in store for you if you say yes, but gave you no true sample of my claims. I'm here to rectify my oversight."

Five

A high-pitched alarm kept clanging in the distance.

Jen vaguely recognized it was logic, reminding her that she hadn't asked her questions, stated her terms or obtained her safeguards.

She let it clamor, then tuned it out. Everything it was yelling about suddenly felt irrelevant. Anything would be when you were drowning. As she was. In Numair.

And he hadn't yet done anything but sweep her up in his arms and claim her lips. If she felt taken, possessed, devoured already, what would she feel like when he fully made love to her?

For the first time in her life, self-preservation wasn't her foremost consideration. She wanted him more than she wanted to be safe. It was insanity and she knew it. She never knowingly did insane stuff. But for him, she'd do anything. With him, she wanted everything.

Suddenly the world gave way beneath her, and she felt she was plummeting. He'd only put her back on her feet.

The only reason she didn't heap to the ground at his feet was because he kept one muscled arm around her waist. It tightened, pulling her against him fully, her toes barely touching the ground. She was totally in his power, loving it and delighting in every hard inch of him that was imprinting her trembling flesh. She moaned when his other hand rose to cup her cheek.

"I spent all night and all day in agony. Tell me you did, too." She could only nod, but her muteness seemed to satisfy him. "And as I suffered, I planned everything I'd do to you, all the ways I'd assuage the hunger, slowly, thoroughly."

She was all for *thoroughly*. But didn't know if she could withstand slowly. The plea to hurry and take her would have spilled from her lips if they weren't trembling out of control with anticipation.

He made it worse, rubbing his thumb against them, his breathing becoming audible, each draw into his endless chest chafing inside her own. "I never knew wanting like this, or anything like you, existed. I thought the ferocity of my desire scared you, that it sent you running away."

She forced words out. "It scared me how much *I* wanted you. I was terrified I was out of my mind."

"You were. As I was. As I still am. As I will remain." His thumb stilled. "Are you still afraid?"

She rubbed her lips against his hard flesh, begging him to continue. "Only that my heart might stop."

Triumph and lust blasted her as he pressed her harder into his length. "I *will* stop your heart. With pleasure."

She nodded, closed her eyes to savor the sensations that emanated from her deepest recesses. She moaned as she caught his tormenting thumb in a nip.

His sharp intake of breath sliced away more of the leashes of her inhibition. She grazed her teeth along his skin, the skin of a seasoned warrior, hardened in battle, scarred in ordeals, healed with limitless stamina and now impervious. She again wondered what kind of life he'd really led. As if tasting him would explain it to her, she suckled him, and his texture and taste only had more moist heat surging in her core.

A fiercer inhalation expanded his chest, crushing her swollen breasts against it. He rubbed against them until she felt they'd burst, the abrasion of his hardness and their clothes turning her nipples into pinpoints of agony. A scalding growl rumbled from his depths as he tugged her thigh around his hips, the hand at her waist securing her there as he ground his erection against her melting core.

She whimpered as he started thrusting against her, at the same time ravaging her neck in suckles she knew would leave their mark. Pleasure hurtled through her blood, making her lightheaded. Her knee buckled, and he picked her up, had her wrapping her other trembling leg around him, letting him have all her weight, making him crush her to him even tighter.

She felt as if her very existence depended on him, his body and breath, his hands and mouth, as he tasted her flesh and took over her will. She was no longer herself, but a mass of need open to him, his to exploit and plunder. There was nothing more to hear but his voracious growls and her thundering blood as he stroked her up and down his body, had her ride his erection through their clothing.

The throbbing between her legs escalated into pounding, and she cried out his name. His torment only increased until she nipped at his lip in her desperation.

"You've got it all wrong." His bass tone made her eyes snap open. "I'm the one who's going to feast on you tonight, wring your magnificent body of every pleasure it's capable of experiencing."

She nodded, her breathing becoming ragged, her lungs

starting to burn. She'd agree to anything he wanted to do to her.

He rested his forehead against hers. "This is unparalleled. Agonizing but sublime."

"Yes," she whispered.

Nothing she'd ever experienced had prepared her for this. For him. She was disintegrating with need, yet she knew this protracted inflammation of their senses would make his eventual lovemaking far more satisfying than a frenzied coupling would have been.

He separated from her, making her cry out again with his loss, but he did so only to press her against the wall. He slid down her body, then, in torturous slowness, rubbed up over her again as he bunched her stretchy dress on the way up. His visual embrace was only interrupted for the seconds it took to sweep the garment over her head.

He set every inch his lips and hands touched on fire before going to her bra's clasp, snapping it undone. She gasped as its constriction eased, then louder at the spike of ferocity in his gaze as he monitored her reaction. He drew more gasps as he caressed her bra loose, then in one silky sweep, he freed her from its bond.

Suddenly, shyness hit her out of nowhere. This man she'd met only last night was here, in her home, just inside her door, and he had her almost naked as he stood fully clothed. It was crazy. It was insanely arousing. And it was the best thing that had ever happened to her. And the most overwhelming.

Before she could snap her arms over her nakedness, he dropped to his knees.

Seeing him kneeling before her, looking up at her with what looked like wonder, her lips dropped open with unbearable stimulation, but no words came out.

It was him who talked. "I thought I knew what I'd find

beneath that dress you hid behind. I was wrong. You're a goddess, Jenan."

This made words of incredulity escape her. "Look who's talking."

"I'm done talking." He tugged her hard to him, rumbling, "Now I worship you."

She would have keeled over him if his shoulders hadn't stopped her forward pitch. He added to her imbalance as he fulfilled his pledge. She whimpered at each kneading of her buttocks, lurched with every tongue thrust into her navel, shook at each drag of teeth across her breasts. Her moans sharpened as he clamped her nipple, until a cry rushed out at his first hard suckle.

"Numair...*please*."

In answer, his thumbs hooked into the top of her panties, peeling them down her shaking legs.

In seconds she was standing in nothing but her sandals, her clothes discarded at her feet. Numair's eyes roamed her every inch as if he would gobble her up.

Everything spun. This was really happening. Numair was really here, and he had her naked. He would take her. And she would let him.

Let him? She wasn't begging him to only because she could barely breathe.

She watched him as if from another realm as his hands closed over each leg in turn and his lips melted down her flesh, kissing and fondling from foot to thigh. Her consciousness flickered like a bulb about to short out.

"The feel of you, the taste and scent of you are perfection, magic. Madness. *Enti jenan ann jadd*."

She gasped. He'd just spoken in her mother tongue. Said that she was truly madness. She'd always hated it when people attributed this meaning to her name. Which they did a lot, as they deemed most of her actions since she'd turned eighteen to be deranged. But the way he said it, the way he meant it… Like everything else, when it was from him, she loved it.

By the time he'd explored her every inch, she'd become a literal puddle. She could feel her arousal running down her thighs, could scent it, and she knew he saw and smelled it, too, from the wildness she felt emanating from him. Then something scalding rumbled from his depths, and he pressed her back, slid her up against the wall, opened her thighs and draped them over his shoulders.

Before she could register his intention, he nudged the lips of her femininity with his nose, rumbling again as he inhaled her deeply, and those rugged fingers caressed them apart, sliding through her molten need. She keened, lurched with jolts of sensation almost too much to bear. Oral sex had left her repulsed or numb before, but not now. With Numair she ached for it. As he dipped a long, powerful finger inside her, each slow inch made her feel how empty she'd been all her life. How only having him inside her would fill the void.

But she wanted *him*, and she tried to tell him by tightening her legs around his head, pulling his hair out of its confinement and dragging him up by it. He only opened her fully and burned her to the core in his ragged hunger.

She malfunctioned completely as his tongue and teeth scorched the heart of her femininity, slowly, thoroughly, as he'd promised. The sight of his magnificent head between her thighs, the knowledge of what he was doing to her was almost more incapacitating than the physical maelstrom.

Through the delirium, she watched him cosset her, strum her, drink her, revel in her need and pleasure. He seemed unable to have enough, and yet to know when she had.

"Now let me see how much I pleasure you."

Just by his demand, by the exact pressure and speed he seemed to know would unravel her, her body heaved in a chain reaction of searing ecstasy. He held her eyes all through it, watching her greedily.

After he'd wrung her of everything her body had to give, she went down like a demolished building all over him. A rough sound of gratification rolled from his gut as he received her collapsing weight effortlessly and stood up.

She flopped in his arms like a rag doll until he whispered in her ear, "Wrap yourself around me, *ya jenani*."

His words injected power into her limp muscles, made her clasp her arms around his shoulders, her thighs around his hips. She would give him anything he wanted.

It was indescribable, being draped around all his power, feeling everything he was encased within her limbs. She now knew she'd been empty and anchorless all her life, would remain so if she couldn't enfold him, hang on to him like this. The thought should have scared the hell out of her, this dependence she was developing unknown to her. It only felt amazing now.

She rested her head against his shoulder as he strode with her clasped tight across her two-room apartment, as if he knew exactly where her bedroom was. Which she wouldn't put past him, to have already obtained the blueprint of this whole building and its unit models. This was a man who was always in the know, about everything and everyone.

She felt as if she was gliding through a dream, her body echoing with the hum of pleasure he'd just given her. And it was as if she was seeing everything for the first time. Everything with him felt new, painted in wonder, infused with magic. And madness. He'd been so absolutely right about that.

As he crossed into her bedroom, she was roused from her delicious lethargy again. Numair had entered her most private place. And she suddenly wished she'd installed so many more lights, so she could revel in every single de-tail of his perfect body when he finally let her see it. As it was, there were only her bedside lamps and two lamp stands in the opposite corners. But she suddenly noticed something else.

Her bold decor in gradations of teaks and greens with accents of ebony seemed to echo his coloring.

Raising her gaze to him as he closed the door, as if he was making sure he had her locked away with him from the world, she melted a caress down his chiseled cheek. "See this place? My inner sanctum?"

His smile was scalding. "It's all you."

"Actually, it's all *you*." His hands tightened on her back and buttocks, his pupils flaring in surprise. She elaborated. "Every color here is yours. Your skin, your eyes, your hair. It's as if I've picked every one to suit you, as a tribute to your beauty. Seems my preference for the color scheme was some kind of prophecy."

His eyes went supernova as he bore down on her against the door he'd just closed. "Everything you say, everything you do, everything about you, sends me out of my mind. Your bill is getting heavier. And I will exact payment in full, *ya galbi*."

She shuddered at the impact of his sensual threat, the sensory overload of being sandwiched between his heat and the cool door, of feeling the steel of his erection nudging her oversensitized intimate flesh.

But it was hearing him call her "my heart" in her mother tongue that tore a sob from her depths, made her drag his head down and crash those cruelly arousing lips down on hers.

When he pulled away, his face had transformed into that of a total predator. "I wasn't exaggerating before. You *are* tampering with my sanity, Jenan. I've never even imagined being out of control. But I am now. So don't touch me again, don't hurry me, don't say a *thing*, if you don't want to have a raving lunatic all over you."

She giggled. "If this is you out of control, I'd hate to see you in it. You'd probably kill me with frustration—"

His lips crashed on hers, swallowing her words.

She'd imagined being kissed since she was old enough to know what kisses were. She'd tried many, many kisses before. It turned out she shouldn't have bothered imagining or trying.

This was a kiss. From those lips. This man. A kiss from now on could only be his, each sweep and thrust burying her under an avalanche of sensations.

Then she was flat on her back, and he was on top of her, like last night. But she was now fully naked and on her bed. And she combusted. She undulated beneath him, writhed, whimpered for him to please, please hurry. But he subdued her, took his time. He held her arms above her head as his other hand flowed down her face, her shoulder, ending up squeezing the aching heaviness of one breast.

His eyes were vehement with warning. "You can't implore me to hurry. You can only moan in pleasure. That's as much as I can endure."

"Let me see you," she moaned.

"You're already breaking the rules."

"You're unfair," she lamented.

"It's your beauty that's unfair."

She tried to free her hands, needing them on any part of him without the barrier of clothes.

He only immobilized her, then, growling deep like a feasting predator, he continued owning her body.

He took her to the brink so many times, until tears slid down the sides of her face and wet her hair. Only then did he come up to straddle her.

He kneaded her breasts, grazed her nipples. "I've never seen or tasted anything so beautiful."

Her hands shook on his belt. "I want to see you—I want you filling me. Please, Numair, please, *now*."

He escaped her flailing efforts, tore off his shoes and socks, then surged up to stand on the bed over her, his endless legs like pillars of a great statue on both sides of her. Then he started stripping, exposing his glory.

She rose to her elbows, gaping at his proportionate perfection, all that rippling power encased in polished teak, accentuated with dark silk. But her heart fisted until it emptied at the evidence of violence he'd suffered. She'd expected he'd led a life full of danger, what had led to his current expertise. But his body painted a far harsher life than she'd even imagined.

A cry spilled from her as she surged up, hands and lips trembling over his scars. Once she'd reached the one just beside his heart, she felt pain echoing what he must have once felt, and tears filled her eyes.

His hand closed over both of hers over his heart. "It was long ago, in another life."

Her tears flowed. "You must have suffered so much…"

"I survived, and it made me stronger." He came down on his knees, dragged her up and crushed her to his length, his lips scorching her face. "And it all brought me here, to this point in time, to you."

What he said was so poignant, the spasm in her chest intensified.

He raised her face to his. "Do my scars repel you?"

That turned off her distress like a tap. "*No*. Like those harsh, merciless things I felt in your nature, these marks of suffering and endurance make you even more unbearably arousing to me. They make me want to devour you even more. Numair—" she moaned between kisses all over him, reaching for the briefs that did nothing to imprison his erection "—you're more beautiful than I even imagined. I want to worship each inch of you."

With a groan of relief, he dodged her groping lips and hands and tore off his briefs in barely leashed ferocity. "Later, *ya hayati*, much later."

Hearing him use another of the lavish endearments used in her region, "my life" this time, made her collapse back on the bed, shaking with anticipation, but also intimidation. She'd never seen anything approaching his girth and length and hardness.

He came down over her again, threaded his fingers through her hair. "Now I take you. And you take me."

Though she doubted she could take him, she arched up into him, held out her trembling arms. "Yes."

He impacted her with his full weight, made her cry out, reveling in how her softness cushioned his hardness.

Perfect. No, sublime. Just like he'd said.

She opened her legs wider, and he guided them over his waist. Then he stilled over her.

Squeezing his eyes, he rose off her to reach for his pants, produced a condom from its back pocket. Tearing the foil with his teeth, he rose on his knees between her splayed thighs and started to roll it over his erection.

His actions finally registered. He was protecting her. He was giving her the choice. And she made it.

Her hand shot out, convulsing over his, stopping his action.

His eyes spewed surprise. "Are you protected?"

She shook her head.

The triumph that flared in his eyes almost knocked her out. "You're saying yes."

She nodded, tears beginning to flow again. She was saying yes to everything. She wanted him to claim her fully, wanted his seed inside her, knowing it would probably take root, hoping with everything in her that it would.

"You don't want to wait? Until after I demonstrate why you should say yes?"

"I had all the demonstrations I need the moment I saw you standing on that threshold last night."

His face seized with such pride and possessiveness, it would have made her run screaming before, but it was exactly what she needed from him now.

Her surrender deepened as he cupped her hips in a huge hand, tilting her, prostrating her. Holding her gaze, he dragged it down to where he held his erection with the other hand. He made her watch as he nudged his scorching crown against the knot where her nerves converged. She rose off the bed on a shrill cry of ecstasy. He slid up and down, circling her quivering bud as he bathed himself in her readiness, until she writhed, her gasps fracturing. Once he'd made sure he'd taken her back to the edge of insanity, he positioned himself at her entrance. Then he plunged inside her, feeling like a newly forged sword just out of the fire.

She screamed at the pain and shock of his invasion.

Even after she'd seen how big he was, she'd hoped it wouldn't hurt too much, since she'd had sex before and she was so ready. But it seemed she couldn't have been ready for him. Nothing would have made her withstand that first thrust. She doubted nothing ever would, that he'd always hurt her at first. And he'd give her unimaginable pleasure in contrast afterward. Even though the pleasure hadn't come yet, she knew it would. And it would be devastating.

On the second thrust, he seemed to realize her pain.

He froze above her, his voice a bass rasp. "Weren't you married before?"

His question elicited an amused huff. "I thought so. Seems I wasn't."

"You're so tight, as if your body was never tried."

"It wasn't. Not by you." She shuddered beneath him, the pain receding, tremors of deep delight starting to seep into the flesh clenched around him. "I do feel it's my first time."

Her actual first time had been nothing like this. It had been a disappointment wrapped in a vague ache. It had been on her wedding night. If it had been before, the marriage itself wouldn't have happened.

"I hurt you." He sounded more distressed than she did.

"Yes." He cursed, tried to pull out of her, but she clung to him inside and out. "You're hurting me so good. The pain is nothing compared to how you feel inside me. I want it to hurt. I want you to brand me."

She clamped his hips in her quaking legs and pulled him deeper. With the action he grew even bigger inside her. Caring nothing that it burned, she thrust her hips upward, engulfing more of him. It was overwhelming, being stretched by him, being filled by him beyond her capacity.

"Give me all of you." She confessed what she'd been thinking right before he came. "Show me no mercy."

"You *do* want a raving lunatic all over you."

"Oh, yes, please."

Instead, he withdrew, and she cried out with his loss, urging him to sink back into her. He resisted her squirming pleas, his shaft resting at her entrance for a moment before he sank slowly back inside her.

On a gust of passion, she opened wider for him. He watched her, gauging her reactions, adjusting his movements to her every gasp and grimace, waiting for the pleasure to submerge the pain before he let her really have all of him, before he showed her no mercy.

"Glorious, *ya galbi*, inside and out." He braced over her on outstretched arms, his muscles bulging, the tendons standing out in his powerful neck. Everything about him confessed his equally agonized pleasure. "So tight, so hot… Jenan…you're burning me."

His face clenched in what did look like suffering as he started pounding into her, forging farther inside her with each plunge.

Then he angled her and sank in her to the hilt. "Burn me, *ya jenani*, consume me as I invade you, take all of me, all the way to the heart of you."

She arched beneath him, thinking he'd reached her heart for real. And he had—the heart of her femininity, her womb. That intimate nudge was beyond anything she'd dreamed of. She'd been resigned to live alone, to never know true intimacy. But now, as he'd promised, every spark of sensation she was capable of feeling gathered into one pinpoint of absolute being, with Numair. Then it exploded.

A stifled shriek tore from her as she shattered around his invasion. She reformed only to splinter again and again around his pounding thickness. Her screams filled her head, accompanying the ecstasy razing her body.

Then his roar drowned everything out as she felt him stiffen in her clutching arms, ramming her deeper than ever before as he spilled into her, his seed filling her.

He was the only man she'd ever let take his full pleasure inside her. But he'd also been the one to give her far more than pleasure. Her first true intimacy.

Her cries stifled as it all finally overwhelmed her, loosened her grip on consciousness...

A sweep of delight cascaded down her back and buttocks then up. Again and again.

Jenan rose slowly from the depths of bliss to the realization that she was being stroked like a feline. And she was lying on top of a great one, who seemed to be purring a deep, deep rumble that vibrated in her bones. The sound was one of absolute satisfaction.

Yeah. She knew exactly how he was feeling. She felt satiated in ways she couldn't have imagined, in perfect peace for the first time in her life.

His lips moved against her forehead. "I trust your two-hour sleep was recharging?"

"Two hours!" She struggled to prop herself over his chest, her hair raining down on it.

His own hair was fanned around his head over a pillow the exact same color of his eyes, making him look like a black-maned lion instead of the sleek, gleaming panther he usually was. She almost collapsed on top of him again.

"Anything to add, besides incredulity at the length of time you were asleep? Although you already said yes, I'm still anxious to know if I delivered on my big promises."

She pulled a face at him, combing her fingers through the luxury of his hair. "If you'd delivered any more, I would have expired. I did for those two hours."

"I did, too."

"You did?"

"I lasted long enough to not crush you beneath me, then all I know is I woke up ten minutes ago to find two hours have passed. Another all-time first."

"This never happened to you?"

"You're the first thing to ever knock me out. And without even trying. I'm starting to worry what you'll do to me when you do try." He shifted, brought her to her side facing him, kissed her deeply, leisurely, then whispered into her lips, "This was, hands down, the best thing that has ever happened to me. *You* are."

She suckled the tongue rubbing against hers, caressed the muscled back rippling with mind-boggling power beneath her fingers, disbelief still reverberating inside her. That she'd found him. That he'd wanted her. That they'd shared all this, a lifetime's worth of events and emotions, in only twenty-four hours. Dare she expect more and even better in the days and weeks to come?

She smiled into his kiss. "Same here. Word for word."

He pulled back to look at her, his own smile bliss and

bedevilment at once as he pressed her flush against him, driving his intact arousal between her thighs. "Not letter for letter?"

"You're too greedy, sir."

"I'm not." As her eyebrow rose in challenge, he kept a straight face as he elaborated, "I'm insatiable."

She laughed. It was such a delight to be exposed once again to that unexpected and unusual sense of humor that was the exact thing to tickle hers.

She wiggled against his erection. "I have rock-solid proof to this claim."

He turned her on her back with a growl before he suddenly stopped. "Have you told your father everything?"

"Since I had no details, I preferred to say nothing."

"So you disappeared from your so-called engagement party, let them all go insane wondering what happened to you, without a word of explanation?"

"Yep, that's it in a nutshell."

His lips suddenly spread into one of those smiles that gave her severe arrhythmia. "I said you were perfection."

She grinned back. "I'm not going to keep saying *look who's talking*. I'll record it so you can play it back whenever needed."

He guffawed, his first full-fledged laugh that she'd heard. Or it might be his first ever, since he looked very surprised, as if it had never happened before.

Yeah, right. He'd lived forty years without laughing from the heart even once?

No matter what, he was laughing from the heart now. She adored the ease and humor that flowed between them, when in her experience, postsex had always been tense and almost hostile. But that had been post–disappointing sex. She'd never known what post-earth-shattering sex was like. Till now.

Before he continued his earlier thought that had been

interrupted, she held him off for one more question. "You haven't told me what you do intend."

He rose on extended arms. Seriousness replaced the mischievous passion in his eyes. "Tell your father to say nothing to Hassan and fly back to Zafrana. We'll meet him there, where I'll convene with him and his cabinet to get the details of the kingdom's problems and debts. I have an idea already, since I spent the past night and day investigating the situation. I expect to set things in motion immediately. Once I do, we'll go to Saraya and disabuse Hassan of his having the upper hand and the title of your fiancé."

Her heart tightening, she stared at him in dismay.

Seeming to realize her distress, his gaze filled with concern. "Are you okay? Are you feeling any pain?"

She shook her head, bit her lip. "Don't get me wrong. I appreciate what you're doing beyond words. I really want this mess over with and Zafrana out of danger. But I really hoped I didn't have to go back again."

His expression cleared then heated, seduction in one lethal package. "But it won't be the same when you go this time." He bore down on her. "This time you'll be with me."

"You expect to carry on our…affair there? You want to kick up a region-wide scandal?"

"I care nothing what others think, as you know, but for your and your family's sake, there won't be a whiff of scandal. I know how to keep a secret."

Still worried, she murmured, "I bet you can."

"Leave everything to me and just concentrate on being totally free, on taking everything you want with me."

When he put it that way, how could she object?

He stabbed his fingers into the hair at her nape, tethering her to the mattress by it, making her gasp then open wide for him, lips and legs. "Say yes, *ya jenani*."

Unable and unwilling to say anything else, she cried out, "Yes!" as he plunged inside her.

And all through the night, she said an inordinate amount of yeses to just about everything, every apprehension evaporating in the conflagration that consumed her body and soul.

<u>Six</u>

"**A**re your sisters to be trusted?"

Jen watched Numair's lips move, and the constant urge to capture them, lose herself in their pleasure and possession, almost overwhelmed her again.

She *had* heard him, understood the individual words, yet couldn't come up with a collective meaning for his question. Her mind's processing powers were busy catapulting back in time to what those lips had been doing to her for the past three days. Day and night and in between. Up till fifteen minutes ago when her sisters had come on board his private jet now sitting on the tarmac.

After that first night in her apartment, he'd taken her back to his suite at The Plaza, and they hadn't left it. They'd done nothing but feast on each other, each time better than the one before it. They'd made love in so many ways she'd never known possible, ways she hadn't dreamed of or thought would be pleasurable. Not until she'd done them with him. She'd been right beyond her wildest dreams.

The incredible being known as Numair was the one man to teach her all there was to know about passion, the one who could plumb her sensual potential. And then some.

He was standing before her, perfection and beyond in a casual black suit and a shirt one hue darker than his eyes. She'd picked it for him, loving how it made his eyes even more incandescent. He was exuding vitality and virility and that all-out hunger that only seemed to increase in his eyes, in his vibe. It made her feel wanted, cherished, limitless.

He now quirked a dense eyebrow as if to prod her… The eyebrow she'd indulged in tracing with her lips and fingers and nibbling with her teeth…

"Jenan?"

"Huh?" was all she finally said.

"I was asking if I can do this…" He cast a quick glance over her head, then scooped her up into the bedroom of his plane, closing the door and pressing her against it. He bore down on her with his bulk and arousal, sank onto her lips. When he raised his head, she was wound around him, arms and legs. His gaze was satisfaction itself as he viewed her blatant arousal and completed his question. "In front of them, and trust them not to out us to the whole world?"

Landing with a thud from euphoria back to reality, she unclamped him from her limbs and found ground again. "I would usually say *el serr fe beir*, or 'the secret is in a well' with them. But then nothing is usual about you. Or us. You are such a huge deal, they've had their jaws on the floor since they've seen you in close quarters. They're bursting at the seams with curiosity about the nature of our relationship and they've already asked me the same question in a hundred different ways, and none of my half-truths have satisfied them. I expect they're going to work on you now in their quest for the truth."

After taking another brief kiss as if he couldn't stop

himself, he said, "How about we appease them, take them into our confidence?"

She licked his lingering taste off her lips before chewing on her lower one. "I usually trust them with anything, but then I never had any secrets for them to keep. They're so used to flaunting my news in everyone's face. I'm sure they'll want to brag about you, and I don't want to put them to such a test. Even if they promise to keep our secret and mean it, you, as you very well know, are too much. You would make anyone break their rules and do things that are totally out of character."

"Anyone, but not you."

She giggled. "You're kidding, right?"

"I'm doing no such thing. You're following every rule you forged for yourself, taking what you believe is right for you without consideration of society's restrictions. Everything you're doing with me is perfectly in character for you. You're enterprising, direct, fearless and a precise judge of character. You knew at once I'm the one for you, and you didn't waste time in empty maneuvers, just took what you want and need."

"When you put it that way, you almost make it sound as if I knew what I was doing."

"You did. You do." After another deep, drowning kiss, he raised his head, ran a coveting finger from her cheek down to the cleavage hidden by her demure, floor-length russet dress. "So will we or won't we?"

"Now that I think of it, with the way they both live online, if we don't want this shared with a few million of their close friends on social media, you won't only be unable to haul me and devour me like you just did, you'll also have to keep your hands to yourself completely."

A thundercloud of a frown came over his face. "Fifteen hours without touching you at all? That's not even a possibility. I only *look* like a superman."

She poked him playfully, found his usually rock-hard abs the consistency of steel. "Relax, or you might snap something. Consider it a chance to find out if abstinence is as good for the soul as it's always advertised."

"Who says I have one?"

She laughed, gave him an exuberant hug. "Since it's something most people are supposed to have, you probably don't, since you can't possibly have something so mundane. Come to think of it, if you don't have a soul, it must be superfluous, since you're perfect just the way you are."

Before he could pounce on her again, she slid through his arms, opened the door and rushed out of the bedroom.

All she wanted was to drag him down on that king-size bed and continue their intimacies. But she half expected her sisters to barge in looking for them. And for answers to their burning curiosities.

In truth, she wished she could tell them, to have it all out in the open. But it was unheard of for a woman from her region to announce that she had a lover. The only accepted relationship was marriage, or the engagement leading to it. Anything else had to be done in secret and never admitted, or it had to look like the accepted cultural format. Her society took hypocrisy so far that it accepted that people who wanted to have a one-night stand or were even paying for sexual favors to resort to *katb el ketab*, or literally "writing the book of matrimony," then divorcing as soon as the next day. *That* was all right with the so-called conservative society. But adults who wanted to be together without social subterfuge? They were punished and persecuted.

No wonder she'd never wanted to come back.

But then if it ever came to a worst-case scenario, she figured Numair was so powerful that even the collective venom of society wouldn't be able to touch her, or her family. He wouldn't let it. Not that she wanted to let it come to that.

He followed her, his tension bombarding her back. It heightened to full blast when Fayza and Zeena's voices rose from the conference/entertainment area they'd been exploring with the flight attendants since coming on board.

She tossed him a teasing smile over her shoulder. "Think of the appetite we'll work up by the time we arrive in Zafrana. I can't wait to see the hideaway you've arranged for us there."

His lips compressed in a severe line. "I'll tell your sisters we're not taking them with us, that another of my jets will fly them back to Zafrana."

Her smile widened before it faltered then disappeared. "You're serious!"

"Fifteen hours without touching you is beyond serious."

She gaped at him. "What excuse could you possibly give for not taking them with us now?"

"That we've had a change of plans and will make long layovers for business purposes in places where they can't go sightseeing or shopping. I'll make them grab gratefully for the direct flight home I'll offer."

"Are you always ready with a convincing story like that?"

His stony scowl told her his mind was made up and wouldn't budge. She still had to try to budge it.

She exhaled. "I really want you to have some time with my sisters, as I doubt you'll see them again alone for any length of time. Put up with the no touching for a few hours, and I'm sure they'll fall asleep at one point. You know I'll race you to bed then. We'll have your flight attendants standing sentry to alert us when they wake up."

His gorgeous lips twisted. "Then what? You'll explode from my arms, jump into your clothes and rush out to pretend you've been out here all along?"

"No, you'll do that." She met his returning scowl with a devilish grin. "You'll pretend you volunteered your room to me."

"You want me to tear myself from your arms because of your sisters, and go out to them? Aren't you afraid I'll eat them?"

She whooped with laughter. "Nah, they're too skinny and cute, and you're used to crunching overfed monsters. You're drafted into service because you can dress far faster than me."

"Only if you're okay with me going out to them in only my pants."

"I sure am not," she exclaimed, her insides tightening yet again at envisioning the sight of him half-naked. "I want their ovaries intact!"

"What ovaries? They're kids."

It again delighted her that he continued to prove he was nothing like other men. She'd seen how men of all ages looked at her gorgeous sisters, caring nothing that they were lusting after girls still in their teens, the age of their daughters or even granddaughters. No matter how they attempted to mask their sexual assessment and coveting, it was always there in their eyes, especially on that first exposure to her sisters' intense natural beauty.

There'd been nothing but neutrality in Numair's eyes and vibe. He considered them just people, who happened to be females, very, very young ones. And it wasn't because he could be old enough to be their father.

Numair didn't define himself according to such trivialities as age, but rather experience, abilities, impact. And in those, he'd sure amassed far more than dozens of successful, influential men his age. He was a man who'd seen and done and fought and triumphed over so much, his soul, or whatever he had that stood for one, was jaded and ancient.

And it made him the be-all and end-all of her fantasies, those she already had or was still forming.

She sighed, running her hands down the chest she'd just imagined naked. "Oh, Numair, you'd endanger any female alive, age notwithstanding. But we will fly my sisters home, and you will not scare them now, nor storm out half-naked and eat them because they woke up and interrupted us."

"How about we get our sentries to stall them until both of us can go out and play this charade for their benefit?"

Intensely pleased he'd started negotiating, she shook her head. "It has to be only you for a very obvious reason. Being made of steel, you don't show the aftereffects of our lovemaking. Apart from not turning into a swollen mass like I do, your hair just falls into this silky swathe no matter how much I mess it up. I need ten minutes minimum to get my hair into a semblance of order."

"Or maybe I can just lace your sisters' food with a sedative and have them sleep throughout the flight."

She guffawed. "Don't mess with such stuff. I might be the one who ends up ingesting the sleeping curse, and then where would you be?"

"In Frustrationland." He exhaled heavily. "Fine. We'll do it your way. But if they don't sleep…"

"They will, they will. They spend half their lives sleeping like cats." At his resigned mutter, she took one of his hands to her lips before placing it on her heart. "Cheer up. This will work beautifully, you'll see."

That incredible emerald of his eyes, what she could look into forever, seemed to catch fire. "Anything with you works beyond beautifully. It's why I'm in such a state."

Scalding joy surged from her depths to drench every nerve ending. It was beyond incredible that he felt as uncontrollably passionate about her as she did about him. Those early days of exquisite intensity were indescribable. And though she didn't hope things would remain on this level, this time of pure passion was worth anything. It would be unforgettable, and she'd cherish it forever.

He gathered her to his hard length, as if he really couldn't withstand not touching her for more than minutes. "I want more of you constantly. I feel vicious toward anything that can deprive me of you even temporarily."

"Think happy thoughts. At least nothing vicious. Zee and Fay can't withstand a drop of your aggression."

"Zee and Fay, eh? You don't expect me to call them that?"

"Why not? And I'm Jen, by the way."

"No. You're Jenan."

Her smile widened at his proprietorial attitude as she again wondered how she adored things from him that she'd abhorred from others. "All my life, when anyone called me Jenan, always meaning madness, they regretted it."

"You're *my* Jenan. *My* madness. Anyone else who trifles with your name and that meaning of it *will* regret it."

"Don't go all Terminator on me, or I will end up without relatives."

"Relatives who provoke you and sneer at your name and character? They certainly deserve terminating."

"Let me fight my own battles, okay?"

His ominous expression eased as he bowed his head in concession. "Until you call on my intervention."

She rewarded his newfound flexibility with a loving nip of his chin. As he groaned, tried to deepen the intimacy, she pulled away with a sigh of regret.

"About Zee and Fay… Since they were babies, they adored that I came up with abbreviations for their names. Especially Fayza. She hates her name even more than I do mine."

"You're more a mother to them than an older sister."

It was a statement. A very astute one. Though the girls'

mother—her stepmother—was alive and well, she wasn't maternal in the least, and she'd left both girls to the care of relatives and hired help from birth. Jen had intervened early, making them her responsibility. Even after she'd left for the States, she'd had them with her there every summer and holiday possible. She sure had the lion's share in raising the girls.

She sighed. "They're my girls. I'm the one who'd do anything at all for them."

Something…enormous flared in his eyes.

She was thinking she'd only guess at its significance, unable to trespass on what felt like an intensely personal reaction, when he ended any speculation.

"I feel the same way about my brothers."

She blinked. "I thought you were an only child."

"I am. Those brothers are ones of my choosing, our bond not one of blood, but forged in trials of fire."

"Your Black Castle partners."

She wasn't asking, just stating. He nodded. She wished he'd elaborate about them, about how he'd chosen them, about their trials.

But she was never one for probing such deep privacies. He'd tell her when and if he wished.

"So Fay and Zee? Will you call them that? For me?"

"For you. You've invoked the binding spell that makes me do anything." Indulgence and self-deprecation twitched on his lips. "No one has ever made me change my mind once it's made up. You're seriously messing with it, *ya jenani.*"

Her heart hitched again. "Only fair, since you're scrambling mine big-time."

He opened his mouth to object, and she rose on tiptoes and closed it with an ardent kiss.

Before he deepened it, she stepped away, giggling. "You probably don't have to worry about them anyway. I bet being exposed to you will excite them so much, they'll be exhausted in a couple of hours."

That lethal smile of his dawned again. "In that case, let's go get those girls of yours, and let me proceed to knock them out of our way."

Giggling again, feeling as though she was perpetually a few inches above ground, she called out to her sisters.

In a minute, Fayza and Zeena came sauntering in, their eyes widening again as they fell on Numair, no doubt stunned all over again by his sheer physical presence.

She understood the feeling exactly. Every single time she looked at him, it was a total shock to her system. Just like that first time. Even more each time.

Numair invited them all to take their seats, then gave the order to take off. Little was said until the jet was done climbing and was cruising almost imperceptibly.

Then Fayza turned to him. "So you're the 'undisclosed businessman' this jet was sold to a couple of months ago."

Numair turned his focus on her, and Jen felt that Fayza regretted inviting it, struggled under its impact.

"I think you have it mistaken with another plane."

"I saw a hundred-million-dollar high-tech customized Boeing 737 in an aviation exhibition in Shanghai, China, unveiled three months ago that looked a lot like it. They said they made a replica for an undisclosed businessman."

Numair gave a slight nod. "I've heard about it, but this jet is two years old, and is a Black Castle Enterprises production."

"You mean your business makes planes, too?" Fayza's eyes widened. "But how does that fit with being one of the world's most important contractors in military intelligence and counterterrorism?"

Numair's gaze sought Jen's, communicating so much in the brief visual embrace. It assured her he was "thinking happy thoughts," as she'd recommended. It also expressed approval of Fay's curiosity and intelligence, but above all appreciation of Jen's efforts in raising her sisters.

Turning his gaze back to Fayza, he said, "You've done your homework, I see."

Fayza looked at Zeena, and the two grinned conspiringly at each other.

It was Zeena who said, "We've been doing Google searches on you since Jen told us you'd be taking us all back to Zafrana on your jet."

"Very efficient of you."

After that kudos, Numair's expression turned enigmatic. Jen couldn't help thinking it made him even more menacing than usual. This man did have something inside him that wasn't a soul. Some spirit of vengeance, maybe.

"But now you know what I am," he drawled. "Weren't you worried about coming to the panther's lair alone?"

"We're not alone," Zee blurted out. "Jen is here."

"You think Jenan can protect you?"

Zee nodded vigorously. "She always has. She'd never let anything bad happen to us."

"Even if you turn out to be some nut," Fayza said. "Jen can take on anyone. She's a black belt in kickboxing."

"Is she, now?" He turned to Jen, his gaze cascading down the body he had an inch-by-inch knowledge of, inspecting the memory of every muscle, sending her hairs standing on end so hard they almost shot out of their roots.

"No, *she* isn't anymore," Jen groaned. "My competing days are long gone. I now kickbox to stave off the march of pounds."

"You're still the best!" Zeena protested.

"She is!" Fayza chorused, looking as if she'd die of chagrin now that Jen had shot down her bragging.

"I'm sure she is," Numair placated them smoothly, before turning back to her again. "I would pay anything for a demonstration of your skills."

Fayza quirked her lips smugly. "You can get one for free. Just make an inappropriate move."

"That's a pity, as I don't make those. My moves are all preemptive."

Zeena giggled. "Those would probably also qualify you for a demonstration."

He turned his burning gaze to Jen. "Would they?"

She pulled a mock challenging face. "Why don't you try one on me and see?"

He shook his head. "I bet you reserve your demonstrations for defending others. A satisfactory one would only be on the girls' behalf, I suspect." He turned his gaze to them, and they visibly shrank back and huddled together like two cornered cats. Suddenly, he laughed. "Relax, Fay, Zee. I promised your big sister I won't eat you."

As the girls' faces brightened at his amusement, she rushed to alleviate the rest of their alarm. "Don't listen to him, girls. He won't abstain from eating you because he promised, but because you're not his staple diet."

Numair's nod was seriousness itself. "It's true. To my species little girls are grass, while we're meat eaters, blood drinkers and bone crushers."

For a moment or two the girls appeared unsure whether he was serious, then they must have decided he was really funny because they burst out laughing.

She noticed that something came into Numair's eyes as he watched them splutter. Like what came into his eyes when she said something that particularly appealed to him or surprised him. It was indulgence—minus the heavily sensual undercurrent, of course. The protector vibe was back full-on.

"Grass!" Fayza howled. "We're grass!"

Numair's lips quirked in response to their hilarity. "Yes. So watch out for the hares and the sheep of this world. They're the real danger."

Which was absolutely right, come to think of it. Ed had definitely been a cross between the two creatures. She still couldn't believe she'd married him. Sure, she'd been rebelling. At Fayza's age, she'd been looking for the opposite of her kingdom's chauvinistic men. But still, Ed? She'd put up with him for six whole months before she'd kicked him out on his ear. She must have had a severe judgment blackout at the time.

"But we're not little girls!" Zeena protested belatedly.

Numair's faint smile was all forbearing. "Oh, yes, you are. You're so little I can barely see you. But you'll soon grow bigger and bigger, and your worries and burdens and responsibilities will grow with you. Being little is good. Savor it for as long as you can."

Her throat tightening with emotion at the direction the conversation had taken, Jen interjected, "They'll always be little, as long as they have their big sister."

"Having a big sister like you is a sure way to remain protected, to never face the world alone."

His eyes held *such* warmth. She'd seen them in every temperature, but that was the hardest hitting yet.

"Were *you* ever little?" Fayza asked, her expression filled with curiosity.

He shrugged. "I didn't get the chance to be."

Jen's throat closed completely at the world of pain hidden behind his words. She'd thought he'd acquired his scars as an adult. But had he? A history of early abuse didn't coincide with what was known of his past. But was it his real past? A man like him could rewrite his history with utmost ease. So had he? And what was his real story? Would he ever tell her?

Seeming unwilling to discuss his past, he said, "About your earlier question, Black Castle Enterprises has companies and businesses that produce everything from screws to planes. We produce all our methods of communication and transportation from start to finish. This way, we get everything done to our specs, and it slashes our cost by two-thirds or more, not to mention it puts us in control of our electronic security and personal safety."

The girls looked even more impressed, if that was possible, as Zeena asked, "So how much did this plane end up costing you?"

"Around fifty million," he said. "It's still a lot, but if I'd bought it at this level, it would have cost a hundred and fifty. It's paid for itself in the past two years with the amount of commuting I did with hundreds of people who are key to my businesses. It seats up to thirty people, and I fly up to two hundred times a year, not to mention the other benefits I reap from it. I didn't get to become a billionaire by splurging on things that cost far more than they're worth and aren't an investment that will pay back in spades for the effort, time and money I put into them."

Fayza chuckled. "Fifty million is pocket change compared to the whopping half a billion one of our region's royals recently paid for his latest private jet."

Numair raised one eyebrow. "I will have to hunt him down and rid the world of his excesses."

Jen covered her forehead theatrically. "Don't give him ideas, girls. If you don't want to get rid of someone for good, don't bring them to Numair's attention."

After the girls laughed, thinking that was an excellent joke, Fayza pursued her line of questioning. "So what's the specs of this jet?"

Numair's answer was immediate, and involved. "It's between a Boeing 737 and 777 in size, but you're excused in thinking it was the first, since seeing the interior without the usual seating doesn't give you an accurate estimate of its size, and it's also a twin jet. It flies seven thousand nautical miles at point eight Mach uninterrupted, or roughly sixteen hours of nonstop flight, before it needs refueling.

It has three sleeping areas, and the meeting area has an internet signal booster, so it's the best place to talk on your smartphones, play on your tablets or work on your computers online. You've seen the entertainment/conferencing system. In case you want to hold a party in the air, just let me know."

Both girls' jaws dropped.

Then Fayza exclaimed, "God, you mean it?"

"Ask Jenan. I never say anything I don't mean."

Jen nodded sagely. "He means it."

The girls squealed with delight, deluged Numair in thanks. Even though they were the daughters of a king, the girls hadn't grown up in anywhere near that level of luxury. Their father would have indulged them even with Zafrana's deteriorating economic conditions, but Jen had made sure he didn't, so they didn't grow up spoiled and desensitized from excess.

But now a little indulging from someone who could so afford it was okay. And how they appreciated it. Numair, on the other hand, didn't seem at ease under the bombardment of their gratitude.

To end the subject, Numair asked Fayza, "So how do you know about that other plane you thought this one was? I didn't realize following the news of aviation exhibitions was among the things a girl your age would be interested in."

Fayza sat forward eagerly. "I want to be a pilot, and I'm interested in everything man-made that flies."

And Jen was doing everything to make sure Fayza realized her dreams and soared as high as she could.

The next second, her heart scattered its beats at his feet as Numair said something to the same effect. "Whatever you need to realize your ambition, I'm at your service."

When the girls realized he indeed meant it, and what it meant for someone of his power to help open closed doors or level road bumps for them wherever they needed, Fayza and Zeena again buried him in delight and gratitude.

Intervening this time, Jen began to interact with the trio more instead of only watching them and contributing to their exchange at key points. Then over an exquisite lunch, the conversation and banter flowed more fluently with every passing second.

The girls of course kept trying to get to the truth of *why* Numair was helping Jen, and by association, them, what was in it for him and what exactly had happened in the past four days. Numair deflected their persistence, gave them answers that were at once true, yet said absolutely nothing of the truth. It was uncanny.

But what most delighted Jen was how Numair, for all his widely known misanthropy and his initial reluctance to have her sisters on board, treated them much like she did, with care and indulgence, albeit with his own version of overwhelming authority and firmness. He acted as she'd always imagined a magnificent older brother would be with them. She knew she was getting way ahead of herself, but she'd stopped worrying about anything that would happen down the road. She'd just enjoy the incredible present.

With that in mind, she threw herself into being with the three people she loved being with most in the world…and hoped her sisters would go to sleep soon.

Numair stood at the top of the stairs of his jet and looked over the land he hadn't set foot on since he was a child. Zafrana. Half of his heritage.

Suddenly, all his senses revved, and he turned to the one who had total dominion over them now. Jenan looked even more breathtaking than ever as she approached him. Together they'd step onto the land she'd relinquished by choice and he'd lost by treachery. He would now reclaim it for himself, and make it a place where she could be happy and fulfilled, a home that deserved her.

Her eyes were full of all the wonders they'd experienced together. But for appearances' sake, so they wouldn't invite people's interference into their new and vital bond, she kept to herself the hands that had sent him mad with desire and ecstasy for four straight days.

He luxuriated in how refreshed and satiated she looked. For the girls *had* slept. They'd woken up only during descent. He'd had Jenan in his arms, under him, all around him, for ten straight hours. Half of the time had been consuming pleasure, and the rest rejuvenating slumber.

When her two sisters stepped out behind them, he turned to look at them. It had surprised him to find himself liking them, needing to please and defend them, and not only because they were her family. They smiled at him with that growing fondness and admiration that so affected him as they all descended the stairs to the limo waiting to take them to the VIP arrivals lounge.

As they entered the lounge, the girls rushed to their friends, who'd come to inspect Numair's jet for the promised in-the-air party. He was exchanging an amused intimate smile with Jenan when a deep voice boomed behind them.

"Jenan."

As they swung around, a man, almost as tall and big as him, was striding toward them, his face tinged with an anxious, angry fire. Numair recognized him at once.

Najeeb Aal Ghaanem. Saraya's crown prince. His cousin and the oldest son of his murderous uncle.

Then Numair's head almost exploded with aggression. Najeeb had reached for Jenan, took her by the shoulders in an urgent grip.

"I cut short my tour as soon as I heard. I went to New York last night but couldn't find you or anyone, couldn't get any reliable account of what happened. I called King Khalil, who told me you were returning home, so I flew here to wait for you." His teeth gritted. "My father has crossed every line this time. I can't apologize enough to you, but you don't need to worry. I'll put a stop to this."

Unable to bear it anymore, Numair clamped his hand around Jenan's arm and pulled her into his side. "*I'll* put a stop to this."

Najeeb blinked, as if it was the first time he'd realized Jenan wasn't alone.

As he made eye contact with him, Numair barely held back from knocking him out. From doing far more. He'd killed many men with one blow when he'd felt none of the blind rage he felt now.

The damn man was not only handsome, he also looked noble, sophisticated, his highborn nature oozing from every pore. And he had this…warmth about him, this heroic vibe to boot.

Everything about him was the very opposite of his own savagery and rawness and coldness. Their radically different lives, what Najeeb's father had been responsible for, were written all over them. And he hated him for it.

But he didn't contemplate killing him for that. It was for daring to lay a hand on her, for calling her Jenan. But most of all, for existing and for suiting her far more than he ever could.

Najeeb's surprise abated, righteous anger flooding over his face in its place. "Who the hell are you?"

Though he knew everything about Najeeb, he growled back, "I ask the questions here. Who the hell are *you*?"

As Najeeb bared his teeth and Numair took a step forward to meet his confrontation head-on, suddenly Jenan stepped between them.

Placing one flat palm on each of their chests, she calmly gave each a firm shove. The action itself, more than the power of it, made each of them stumble a step back, severing the chain reaction of aggression.

Looking from Numair to Najeeb, she smiled with mock demure sweetness. "Let this little, helpless, has-no-say woman make the introductions. Numair, meet Najeeb Aal Ghaanem, Saraya's crown prince and my fiancé's oldest son. Najeeb, meet Numair Al Aswad, mega intelligence and counterterrorism mogul…and my lover."

Seven

Jen looked coolly between the two towering hunks who flanked her as they relinquished their visual and verbal duel and turned to gape at her.

Yep. She'd sure managed to shock them out of the impending explosion that had almost ignited out of nowhere.

Anyone might think she was insane, insisting on hiding the truth from her sisters, then blurting it out like that to Najeeb on sight. But though she hadn't really given it any thought before doing it, she did think with Najeeb, the secret would certainly be in a bottomless well.

Najeeb was the most honorable person she'd ever known. Since she'd been a child, she'd always looked up to him, wished they could be closer. For he was exactly the older brother she'd always wished she'd had.

That was why she knew she could tell him anything. Najeeb was the material the knights of old had been made of. Those who would lay down their lives for you once you had their alliance.

Not that she wanted anything anywhere near that drastic from him. She just wanted to come clean to someone about her and Numair. Najeeb was the only one she could think of whom she could tell anything to and trust he'd never expose it at whatever price to himself.

Najeeb, surprisingly, was the first to recover from her bombshell. His gaze couldn't decide what to be—stunned or amused. "Okay, Jenan, you achieved your purpose. You stopped me in my tracks. Very efficiently. I'm sorry I flew off the handle, but I was livid since I heard what my father made you agree to. I was ready to strike out at anything—" he flicked a withering glance at Numair "—or anyone in my path."

Great. Najeeb had jumped right into denial, while Numair was over his surprise and seemed to grow bigger with Najeeb's every word. The danger levels emanating from him entered a critical stage.

She sighed. "I did want to shock you into stopping, and that's why I resorted to the truth. It's always more shocking than any fabrication."

Najeeb looked disbelieving for a few more moments, before he choked, "You're not joking?"

"To borrow a favorite line from someone who's standing right here, I've never been more serious."

"How…?" He paused then realization dawned like a fireball in his sunlit eyes. He looked back at Numair with hostility turning to horror. "You're Numair Al Aswad!"

"So now you recognize me."

"Now I wish I don't." Najeeb turned to Jen in dismay. "How on earth did you get mixed up with a man like him?"

Something scary rolled from Numair's gut. "You have questions, you have anything to say, you talk to me."

Jen raised her hands. "Boys, please, hold your testosterone missiles. I'm standing right in the middle, and your aggression is literally turning my stomach."

Both men apologized simultaneously, stopped, glared at each other, started again, overlapped each other's words again, then fell silent. They stood there seething with frustration as they summed each other up. And she saw something she hadn't realized before.

They looked *so* much alike.

If she'd been meeting them for the first time, she would have thought they were blood relatives, even brothers.

Apart from Najeeb having hazel eyes and close-cropped hair, what really distinguished them wasn't genetic, but the result of their radically different characters and paths in life. Najeeb lacked the harshness that etched Numair's features, the ruthless shrewdness that emanated from him. And while both men were almost the same breadth and height, their bodies displayed the difference between the supremely fit and powerful man that Najeeb was and the lethal juggernaut that Numair was.

But those differences only made them feel more kindred. She couldn't explain why she felt that, but she did. And suddenly this whole situation became untenable.

As the men started arguing again, she clamped each by his arm. "Will you stop alarming everyone in a mile's radius?" She looked from one to the other as they brooded down at her. "Can we now go have this out somewhere private, or do we need some internationally sanctioned neutral ground and peacekeeping forces to keep you two in line?"

They ended up in Numair's place.

The "hideaway" he'd prepared for them. With no roads leading to it, the only transportation was by helicopter.

Though she'd lived in a royal palace, this place still stunned her. She couldn't believe she hadn't even known it existed in her own homeland.

Contributing to the uniqueness of this resort-size property was its seclusion. For a hundred square miles she saw nothing but desert conservation land all around.

Once they'd entered through the semifinished palm wood and bronze gates into this desert paradise, she felt they hadn't only left city life behind, but modern life altogether, too. The understated luxury was so at one with the environment, the villa lacked any trace of the artificial elements that had always put her off in the opulent places she'd been in in Zafrana, from the palace to the houses of the nobility and big businessmen. While all those places strived to belong to an era in architecture and decoration, this place had a timelessness about it.

It was made of the desert, its materials, its color palette, of its majesty and tranquility. Of the many things that took her breath away were the free-roaming oryx and gazelles just outside the gates, and the incredible infinity pool at the back of the sprawling villa. It looked like a swimming pool at its near end, with mosaic walls, steps and ledges in blues and greens, but on its far end it looked like a spring, like those found in major oases, its edge seeming to abruptly disappear into another realm. A mile-long barricade of palm trees separated the back of the property from the rest of the desert that stretched in gently undulating dunes all the way to the Anshar mountains on the horizon.

Inside the villa, spaces flowed onto each other; balcony doors opened to all directions. Every surface was made of stone, colored glass and bronze, and all the furniture and upholstery handmade, everything in warm earth tones, with russets and reds adding splashes of vividness. The whole place felt like an escape into a mystical retreat of solitude.

Numair had somehow read her every preference, even those she'd never fully formulated. He'd known what would most delight her. And in those short days while he'd been always with her, he'd searched for it, found it and acquired it. She didn't think this property was a lease. He moved around here with the assurance of someone who owned the place, even though it was his first time here. The one who'd flown here to close the deal, who now showed them around, was his right-hand man, Ameen. But then, Numair entered any place and owned it, and the people in it.

She couldn't wait to be alone here with him. But for now she had to resolve this issue with Najeeb. Most important, she had to give it her best shot to fix that inexplicably catastrophic first impression between him and Numair.

Now Ameen left their trio in the great space that had many sitting areas, a dining room and four stone fireplaces. Numair handed her down on one of the divans strewn in pillows covered in hand-woven wool in colorful, geometric Zafranian designs. She tried to catch his eyes, exchange the intimacy they'd been reveling in since their first night together. But his focus was trained on Najeeb.

It was beyond clear he abhorred having Najeeb around. And he wasn't thrilled with her, either, right now. He'd bowed to her wishes when she'd invoked what he called her binding spell, suppressing his aversion and inviting Najeeb here. But he wasn't about to pretend he was okay with it.

It baffled her that his vexation with Najeeb hadn't only persisted but seemed to be intensifying.

The two men had gotten off on the wrong foot, both of them having been in a volatile state. Najeeb had already been outraged and easily triggered by a strange man's contention. And Numair, in the acute stage of excessive passion, had his territorial instincts at high alert. With both of their alpha-male levels at the maximum, a locking of horns had been inevitable, and the situation had shot to the danger zone with a few aggressive words.

But while Najeeb had reverted to his usual self-possession and equanimity, Numair's hostility was still building.

Not that he displayed any aggression. On the surface he

was even more neutral than Najeeb, coldly assessing. But she now had a direct line to his inner feelings. She felt a volcano seething inside him.

As soon as they were all seated, with her facing both men, Najeeb left the visual wrestling match with Numair and turned to her. "I'm all ears."

Filling her lungs with air, she let it all out in a long exhalation. "What do you want to hear?"

"The truth."

"I told you that right off the bat. But if you want it in chronological order, here's a rundown of how things happened. You refused to be bundled with me in a marriage of state to serve your father's expansion plans, and disappeared. He decided he'd do what you wouldn't and marry me himself. He cornered my father, and my father in turn threw the ball in my court. I had to pick up the ball, since I knew if I didn't, one of my sisters would be forced to. Then came that fateful evening five days ago, and I met Numair. The rest I already told you."

"*Ya Ullah*, I leave for a couple of weeks, and this happens." Najeeb seemed to struggle to process the events his father had set in motion, his fury again rising. Then suddenly his face turned into a mask of righteous rage. "Back in the airport, he said he'd put a stop to this. Is this what he promised you in return for becoming his lover? Is this how he forced you into his bed so soon?"

Before she could say anything, Numair said in a seething tone, "*He* doesn't coerce women into sex. And suggesting that I have is an insult to Jenan. She would never be coerced into anything like that for any reason."

Najeeb turned his wrath on Numair. "Jenan is a hero, and would pay any price to save her loved ones. She *was* being coerced to marry my father for their sakes."

"*She* is sitting right here." Jen exhaled. "How about we talk *to* each other?" She looked at Najeeb. "I am with Numair because I want to be, because I want him. I hope this answers your questions and closes this subject."

Najeeb stared at her, evidently still stunned that she was talking so openly about her affair with Numair, that dangerous stranger he seemed to know even more about than she did. They'd never talked about anything that even neared such candor and sensitivity.

But he was one of the most flexible, progressive people she'd ever met, and she'd always known that if she needed, she'd be able to talk to him about anything.

He finally nodded. "You're one of the most enterprising and advanced people I know, Jenan." A huff of surprise escaped her. Good to know they held each other in equal regard. Without inquiring about her amusement, he went on, "For a woman from our region to achieve what you have, you had to be far more powerful than a man who achieves the same things. I always admired your strength and will, how you escaped the shackles of your status and stood in the face of our culture's condemnation and our society's persecution. I'm proud of everything you've achieved, and I am proud that your decisions and actions have always proved to be the best thing for you. I also always thought you a most astute judge of character. But I won't lie and say I'm not skeptical this time."

"You think I don't know what I'm doing, huh?" She shrugged. "It's your prerogative to feel any way you want about this, and it's mine to do as I want—and being with Numair is certainly what I want. I only ask that you keep what I divulged to you to yourself, until further notice."

"If you don't want others to know, maybe it's an indication that you feel it might be wrong."

"C'mon, Najeeb, you know better than that. In our region it's best to hide anything you truly care about. People have no concept of boundaries, and they swarm over anything that's made public knowledge, thinking it their right to poke and prod, to interpret it according to their own set of narrow-minded values, to cheapen and sabotage it. You know that when it comes to me alone, I care nothing about what people think, that I always announced all of my tradition-busting decisions before, but this time—"

Najeeb raised his hand. "You don't need to convince me of anything, or to even ask me to keep what you told me a secret. There was never a possibility I'd share anything you told me or anything I find out about you on my own."

Her lips spread. "Why do you think I told you in the first place when I didn't even tell my sisters?"

Alarm spread over his painstakingly sculpted face. "Don't even think of telling them. They and their friends must be speculating enough as it is just seeing you with him. Don't add fuel to the fire by any confirmations."

She chuckled. "Just what I thought, and that's why only you know."

He exhaled heavily. "*Aih.* Only I know. *Ya Ullah, ya Jenan...* I only hope you won't live to regret this, and it won't come at as big a price as I fear."

She felt another wave of aggression blast from Numair, but when he spoke his voice was chillingly calm. "So you've changed your strategy. Now that you failed to shame her or make her doubt her decision, you're trying to plant fear of me in her heart."

Najeeb regarded him with the same arctic composure. "If she doesn't fear you, then she doesn't know what you really are. You, Mr. Al Aswad, are a man to be dreaded. A man to avoid at all costs."

Numair inclined his head. "You're absolutely right, Prince Aal Ghaanem. I am far more than that. With anyone but Jenan."

It was clear Najeeb got Numair's message loud and clear, that he was foremost among the *anyones* who should dread and avoid him. From Najeeb's nonchalance, he was answering with his own unspoken "Anyone but me, buster."

Out loud he said, "You're saying you're changing your ways for her? Or that you're different with her?" Najeeb turned to her, his eyes reproachful. "And you fell for that?"

In one of those imperceptible moves, Numair was sitting on the edge of his seat, like a crouched panther seconds from a neck-gouging attack. "I said you talk to me. I won't say it again."

"How about you keep your threats to anyone who might actually give a damn about them, Mr. Al Aswad?"

"If you don't, Prince Aal Ghaanem, then you don't know what I really am as well as you think you do."

"And it's clear you know nothing about me if you think you can get away with threatening me."

Having heard enough, Jen surged to her feet. "Okay, my neck is really starting to hurt watching your delightful volleys." She planted her fists at her waist. "May I interject with a tiny reminder that you gentlemen are on the same side?"

Numair and Najeeb turned to her in surprise and not a little affront at her suggestion.

An incredulous chuckle burst from her. "*Ya Ullah*, you're both so busy posturing and being macho and trying to wrestle each other under the table that you didn't stop to realize that." At their darkening scowls, she sighed. "I hate to break it to you, but you are. You both want to stop Hassan's nefarious plot and help Zafrana get out from under his thumb. And most important, you both want what's best for me." At their stubborn irresponsiveness, she prodded. "You do both want what's best for me, right?"

"You know that I…"

"You know that I…"

As soon as both men realized they were chorusing their response, they flung each other furious glances.

And she burst out laughing. "See? You not only want the same thing, you're saying the exact same thing, too." At their continued belligerence, she sighed again. "If you both do want my best, promise me you'll stop making me worry you'll tear each other apart the moment I turn my back. Do I have your words?"

Najeeb again surprised her, being the one who nodded first. She'd expected it would be Numair who'd rush to give her what she wanted. It seemed his antipathy toward Najeeb was messing with his priorities. Weird.

But he at last nodded, his voice bottomless, his gaze filled with unfathomable things as he said, "For you."

His response was still disturbing in every way possible, but it was enough for her current purposes. She knew he'd abide by whatever word he gave her.

She looked at each of them. "Since I'm the one with the most at stake here, in every way possible, how about you let me steer this conversation?" They both nodded at once this time. Her heart lifted at the progress. Wishing those two would realize they should be allies, she grinned from one man to the other. "I know both of you planned to be the one to resolve this crisis, so how about we discuss how you intended to do that? Maybe you can jointly devise an even more efficient way?"

"My plan doesn't need any boosts in efficiency," Najeeb said. "I'll force my father to back down."

Numair looked at Najeeb, his lips twisting in irony. "What a coincidence. That is exactly my plan."

Jen's laugh rang out again. "See? You two are so alike, you're almost twins." As their faces darkened again at her assertion, she placated them. "Not that either of you can see or admit it now, but one day you'll realize I'm right. And boy, will I enjoy saying I told you so. But since we have more pressing issues at hand, and you at least admitted you share a common goal, how about you share the specifics of your plans to force Hassan to back down?"

Neither man ended up sharing the specifics of his plan. Or made any promise to work with the other, either.

But at least the hostility that had erupted between them had subsided.

At least it had on Najeeb's side. As for Numair, it seemed as if an impenetrable shield had come down around him, stopping her from reading his thoughts or sensing his feelings, leaving her wondering what their truths were. But she couldn't ask. Not because Najeeb was around, but because she'd never probe into private stuff Numair didn't volunteer.

Najeeb, on the other hand, was a totally different matter. She'd insisted he stay and share their dinner, and he'd accepted her invitation, gradually relaxing in their company. Shedding his confrontational attitude, he'd asked Numair informed, in-depth questions about his work, seeming genuinely interested, then impressed. He had even ended up asking if Numair could use his unique experience and influence to collaborate with him in his humanitarian efforts. Numair had seemed reluctant to give any answer. She felt it was not because he didn't want to help, but because it would involve him with Najeeb. But Najeeb was a master negotiator and had somehow managed to extract a promise from him.

By the time she'd seen Najeeb out alone, as Numair had taken an important and long call, Najeeb had given her his verdict on Numair.

He was big enough to admit he'd been wrong. Both his opinion of Numair and their relationship had changed radically. He'd said he knew men, could sense any sign of sleaze, exploitation or mistreatment a mile away. And he'd seen and sensed only respect and consideration in

Numair's treatment of her. He'd also felt how passionate Numair was about her, and how protective.

Before he'd crossed to the massive clearance where the helicopter had been waiting to take him back to the airport, Najeeb had laughingly said it looked like the Black Panther of Black Castle had finally found the one to tame him. He'd always heard that the most dangerous predators, once tamed, made the best lap cats.

"I thought he'd never leave."

Jen yelped in delight as Numair did this incredible thing he always did. He appeared out of thin air and snatched her off her feet with the utmost ease, then drowned her in the staggering, cherishing power of his embrace.

She clung to him with everything in her as he strode eagerly with her across this unique place, nuzzling her face and lips into the power of his warm neck. At the villa's far end, they entered the most stunning bedroom suite she'd ever seen. Though they were totally alone now, Numair still kicked the door closed, as he always did.

As he crossed to the king-size bed, she took in the tasteful decorations in what looked like authentic Zafranian antiques and handcrafted furnishings. Painted glass and copper lanterns hung from heavy chains, while complementing sconces hung on the walls. Bedouin jars and vases in varying sizes lay on shelves and tables and stood beside the heavy mahogany doors leading to the suite's bathroom and dressing rooms. A braided-wood-and-straw chest sat at the end of the bed, while sofas with the same design and materials and ornate stone-and-bronze tables filled the sitting area facing the balcony doors. All over the floors and even on select places on the walls were hand-woven carpets in the deepest reds, honeys and browns, the same hues of the whole villa. And she suddenly realized.

All the colors in this place were hers!

She'd at first thought he'd bought this place furnished.

But this was too specific to be a coincidence. He had to have done this for her, an answer to her bedroom in New York. But she couldn't even imagine how and when he'd managed to order it done, and no doubt to oversee its realization to his precise vision. It was another proof that Numair was even more powerful than she could imagine.

But he'd taken it beyond matching her coloring. There were other incredible touches. For instance, binoculars on one table and a telescope by the balcony doors, to watch the animals in the morning and the stars at night. But what touched her to her core, had tears surging in her eyes, was an easel with every kind of canvas and paper and art material neatly stacked next to it.

She painted, and he must have noticed that most of the paintings hanging in her Tribeca apartment were desert landscapes. Anticipating that being here would stir her creativity again, he'd provided her with the means to indulge it whenever the mood struck.

Before she could thank him for being so unbelievably thoughtful, he passed the bed, opened the balcony doors and stepped outside to a wooden deck overlooking another, smaller infinity pool. By day the pool would spill out into a never-ending vista of the dramatic desert views. It was now a glittering turquoise splash in a night lit only by a nascent crescent moon and an explosion of sparkling stars. Numair wanted to make love out in the open, with only the canopy of sky and stars for cover.

In the middle of the expansive deck, a gigantic mattress was spread in covers the same deep mahogany red of her hair. He kneeled on it with her still securely held in his arms and tore the covers away before placing her down on the crisp cream sheets and coming down on top of her.

Crying out with the overload of emotions and sensations, she wrapped her arms and legs around him, her breath hitching, her body trembling, molten. It had been twelve hours since he'd made love to her, but with the way her senses were clamoring, ready and on the verge of combusting with his every touch, it felt like twelve days.

His hands alone possessed the ability to dissolve her shackles and release her potential, to expose her to his transfiguring appreciation. In a few hammering heartbeats, he had her open to his desire, making her all-powerful with it. Then his lips and tongue and teeth were all over her, making her feel as he always did, savored and worshipped and devoured.

Then he rose to expose himself to her hunger. She lay there unable to move with craving, her night-adjusted vision luxuriating in his star-silvered perfection.

He kneeled before her and she reached to caress his manhood. Hard and engorged, it felt as if it had been chiseled by virility gods and gifted with endless stamina and discipline. As her hands failed to span his incredible girth and length, the now-accustomed-to thrill of intimidation rattled through her. It again awed her that her hunger was so vast it enabled her to contain that much demand.

In response to her ministrations, his fingers shook in her hair and his formidable body trembled over hers. Her heart expanded. Loss of control wouldn't mean a thing from anyone else. But from Numair, with his supreme sufficiency and restraint, such a demonstration of dependence, such a confession of need, was profound.

What she felt was no longer about hunger, if it had ever been. The need had become all about him and being merged with him.

She cried out her desperation. "Numair, fill me…"

By the golden lights coming from the bedroom and the silver of the moon and stars, she saw the sequence of emotions unspooling across his face as her plea shattered him. He bore down on her, opened her wide around his hips, raised hers off the bed. He held her in one hand, the other supporting himself as he rose halfway on both knees. Then he plunged inside her.

Her scream at his abrupt invasion didn't alarm him now. For he knew that she was yearning for the full power of his flesh in hers, the mutual domination and captivation. And he gave it all to her. He slammed into her, and she screamed for more, knowing he had more, as long as she could survive.

Then too soon, the tidal wave was cresting. Feeling her mounting distress, he rose on extended arms over her. Her gaze clung to his as he burned her with his greed for her total surrender and pleasure. When she started pleading, he angled his thrusts and sent her over the top.

Orgasms crashed through her, over and over, ebbing and cresting again and again. His mouth milked hers for each last stifled scream as she bucked and heaved beneath him, his growls that of the predator he was. On the jet, after their last explosive coupling, he'd said he'd end up dying in her arms of a pleasure overdose. Every time with him felt as if his prophecy would come to pass. What an ecstatic end that would be.

Once she subsided beneath him, he stopped for a while then started again, building his rhythm and her desperation until she pleaded for him to plunge with her this time into the abyss of ecstasy.

Growling with satisfaction at her resurrected hunger, then with his own desperation for release, he let himself go and climaxed inside her. His buttocks tightened hard as he lodged himself into her womb and let loose the jets of completion, roaring his pleasure, his surrender to this overpowering need between them.

The sensation of his release inside her, the intimacy of it, the hope that it would implant the miracle of a life they both wanted to make together... Everything over-

loaded her system into another orgasm. One more powerful than the last.

She surrendered to the ultimate pleasure, and the world
faded away, as usual, nothing remaining in existence but
him and being merged with him...

When she stirred from blissful oblivion, she found herself over him, beneath thick covers, with the balmy desert
night sifting through her hair.

Without moving, she pressed her lips over his heart.

"Thank you."

A deep chuckle reverberated beneath her ear. "Thanks
are certainly mutual here."

"I'm not thanking you for driving me out of my mind
with pleasure. Mere *thanks* doesn't do justice to what you
do to me."

He turned her on her side so he could look down at her.
"Then what are you thanking me for?"

"You should be asking, what *not* for." At his uncom-
prehending frown, she nipped his rugged jaw, delighting
in how his beard bristled against her teeth. He'd shaved
before they'd disembarked from his jet, but a dark stubble
had grown out again. "You really have to work on being
able to accept gratitude and take your dues."

"Whatever you think I did..."

Her kiss sealed his lips, stopped his argument. "What
you keep doing is not a matter of opinion, but facts as solid
and as wonderful as every inch of you."

His groan filled her lungs as she ran her hands down
every one of those inches she had access to. "Anything I do
for you is my absolute privilege and my intense pleasure."

Her passion-swollen lips spread into a grin. "Fine, but
I still get the privilege and pleasure of thanking you, all
the time, so get used to it."

He looked down at her thoughtfully. "I thought you

didn't have much to thank me for today. You evidently consider Najeeb a dear and valued friend, and I jumped down his throat, and I didn't warm to him for the hours he stayed here. I was a lousy host."

"I already knew you don't do warm, Numair, and are not one for social graces."

The power and bulk pressed to her turned to steel. "Like Najeeb, you mean? The perfect gentleman? The living, breathing epitome of the knight in shining armor?"

Her eyes widened as realization suddenly hit her. "Was that what this was all about? You were jealous?"

His eyes blazed into hers. "Insanely." He raised a brow at her. "Perhaps even murderously."

Her mouth dropped open before she exclaimed, "But we're like brother and sister. We refused to even consider marrying each other, triggering this whole mess."

"I knew that, on a logical level. But there was no reasoning with the beast who could only see that his mate was so at ease with someone else." As she shuddered in delight at the word *mate*, he wrapped her hair around his hand and took it to his lips, caressing it as he would her mouth. "I could *feel* your history, your long years of knowledge and understanding, and I suddenly felt like an outsider."

Was that insecurity that came into his eyes? Numair? Was it even possible?

Unable to bear that he'd feel anything bad on her account, she pulled him closer. "My brief days with you mean far more to me than all the years I've had with most people in my life put together. I've come closer to you than I have to anyone I've known my whole life. And I never wanted a gentleman or a knight in shining armor. I want you, the man I knew from the first glance was a ruthless marauder in darkest armor."

His chest expanded, pressing into her sensitive nipples, his darkened eyes brightening again. "So you're not disappointed with me for being the cold bastard that I was with your friend?"

"You can't help what you feel, but you did what I asked. You stopped antagonizing him, invited him here to your place, even when you wanted me here alone this first time—"

He swept her to her back and loomed over her. "And every time. From now on, Ameen will only come when we leave, to clean and maintain the place. But while we're together, no one else will ever set foot here. And it's *our* place, not mine. In fact, since I acquired this place for you, it's yours."

She blinked. "What do you mean acquired it for me?"

"I mean I wrote it in your name."

She jackknifed, sitting up. "What?"

He leaned back on one elbow, indulgence playing on his lips. "I have a copy of the deed here, and another has been sent to your legal representative. This place is all yours, all you. All I ask for is the privilege and pleasure of sharing it with you."

Unable to wrap her mind around the enormity of his gesture, she could only stammer, "But…but…"

He pushed her down again, pressed his lips to hers in a silencing, drowning kiss.

By the time he raised his head, hers was spinning, with everything he was, everything he'd been doing to her and for her. Then his next words made the whole world spin.

"Tomorrow I go resolve your father's and your kingdom's crisis. Now sleep with me under the stars, in this paradise where only we exist, *ya habibati*."

She surrendered to him as he adjusted their position for comfort, secured the covers over them and fell silent. In a minute she was certain he'd fallen asleep.

But there was no way she could, too. Every time she

replayed his last words in her mind, she could barely breathe.

He'd said *ya habibati*.

When he wasn't in the throes of passion.

My darling. My love.

Eight

"You should have told me I'd meet you on a *One Thousand and One Nights* set. I would have come in costume."

Numair stared at the man who approached him as he stood at the top of the stairs facing the helipad. The last man on earth he'd ever thought would come to his assistance. Richard Graves.

The Englishman had waited until the helicopter's rotors had stopped before he talked to make sure Numair heard his mockery. As if Numair didn't already know it was his default in general, and with him in specific.

Only two years older than himself, Richard had been Cobra to him for the sixteen years he'd known him in the prison of The Organization.

But he wasn't one of his brothers. He'd been one of his jailers. He'd long been his nemesis. He was now his partner. It was…complicated.

Richard was now looking around the expansive desert vista surrounding Numair's home.

Yes, his home. That was what this place had become in the past six weeks. His first home. Anywhere Jenan was with him, even part-time like now—when she spent most of the days with him, making love, conducting their businesses remotely, just being together, but spent the nights in the royal palace for appearances' sake—would now always be home to him.

She was home.

"So you've finally found your roots, eh? Happy now?" Richard drawled as he came to stand eye to eye with him. He was the only one who'd ever matched him in strength, in power, in danger and ruthlessness.

Numair glared at the man he'd loathed for the past twenty-five years. The man who'd once been his best friend.

Not that they'd ever mentioned this brief period when they'd been the most important person to each other. Not between themselves, and certainly not to others. All his Black Castle brothers knew was that they were sworn enemies. His brothers had spent the past two decades wondering and asking why. But neither he nor Richard had ever volunteered an explanation. What had happened between him and Richard had been before he'd made the others his team. And it had been unforgivable. Richard should be grateful Numair hadn't killed him the moment he could.

And he would have if not for Rafael Salazar, his youngest brother. Richard had been Rafael's handler, and Rafael had formed an unbreakable bond with him, considered him his mentor, his older brother, even. When Richard had left The Organization and caught up with them by tracing Rafael, Numair and the rest had unanimously decided to eliminate him. They'd considered him the enemy, and a lethal threat to their new identities. Exposure as the agents who'd escaped The Organization would have meant their certain deaths. Or at least being forced to relinquish the identities they'd gone to so much trouble to create.

It had been a simple equation. Richard or them.

But Rafael had put himself between them, insisted he trusted Richard with his life and theirs, that if they got rid of Richard, they had to get rid of him, too.

Rafael's adamant position had forced them to trust his judgment as they always had, and to back down. Not that Richard had made that easy. He'd taunted them, warning them that in a confrontation between all of them and only him, they would be the ones in danger.

Rafael seemed to have called it right, since Richard hadn't exposed them. But Numair suspected it had only been because Richard considered Rafael his younger brother, had killed and would die for him and wouldn't risk him being taken down with them. Numair had wanted nothing more to do with that bastard. But he'd soon found himself forced to collaborate with him in building Black Castle Enterprises.

Being pragmatic, he'd known only Richard had the knowledge, skills and power he needed to construct something impregnable. His own field was military intelligence, espionage and counterterrorism, putting him in position to deal with the huge political and criminal issues that faced a corporation of their size and reach. But Richard was the one who was an incomparable security specialist, who dealt with the everyday dangers, the security issues in the real and cyber worlds that could bring any business down.

So they'd become, for all intents and purposes, partners. Not that this had changed their personal position. They would always remain antagonists.

Richard's lips twisted as he returned his antipathy, just with his usual sarcasm. "I should have known you came from such a land, where vendettas are inherited and cherished as the source of honor and glory. You can't help what you are, it seems. It's in your genes."

Usually, he engaged Richard in the rituals of their ongoing cold war. But Numair couldn't afford to do that now. Not when that damned snake had something he needed.

Knowing that, and determined to make the most of Numair's inability to react as he wished to, Richard smiled like the serpent he was.

Pushing the jacket of his handmade sand-colored suit out of the way, he shoved one hand into his pants' pocket, with the other one still holding the briefcase he was here to deliver. Without attempting to give it to him, he looked around like someone assessing a pawned property he'd come to acquire in lieu of an unpaid debt.

"So I see you installed yourself in a setting appropriate to your future lofty status, until you take over Saraya's royal palace." Richard gave him a baiting glance, one of the staple methods of interaction between them. "You even acquired yourself a local princess."

Numair bristled but forced himself not to flay Richard alive. He wanted that briefcase with a minimum of fuss.

Obviously, Richard had other plans, as his goading intensified. "At first I thought you were stringing her along to spoil Hassan's marriage plans. I thought you'd asked me for help with the release of Zafrana's financial assets to deprive him of his power over Zafrana, to contribute to crippling him before you struck him down. But then you continued carrying on with her, and I realized your actions have all been directed to making *her* and her father indebted to you, and dependent on you. You don't only want Saraya's throne, you want Zafrana's, too. And she's your ticket to it."

This made Numair relinquish any thoughts of restraint. He grabbed Richard's arm with a force that had broken lesser men's arms. "Keep your realizations and theories to yourself, Cobra, and don't even *think* of Jenan again."

Richard's eyes widened, with surprise not pain, the caustic derision disappearing from his expression, contemplative scrutiny descending in its place.

Then he grimaced. "By God, not you, too, Phantom."

Numair knew exactly what Richard meant. Two of Numair's brothers had already succumbed to what they'd all previously considered an ailment none of them was susceptible to. Love. Rafael had married the daughter of the man he'd thought had sold him to The Organization, and Raiden had married the woman who'd once been sent by his former handler to expose him.

But if there was anyone they'd all thought was 100 percent impervious to any emotions, let alone love, it was Numair. And his current companion, of course.

Richard said exactly that. "Besides me, you're the literal last man on earth I expected to fall in love."

If Richard expected him to deny it, to consider it a weakness he wouldn't admit to anyone, most of all to his lifelong nemesis, he had another think coming. The moment he could, he'd shout it from the rooftops if need be. He'd made his peace with the life-changing realization.

He *had* fallen in love with Jenan.

But even that statement wasn't accurate. He'd far more than fallen in love with her. He felt as if she'd become an extension of his being, the most vital part that he'd perish without. Dependence on someone else had been unimaginable before; absolute self-sufficiency had been the basic fact on which he'd built his whole life. Even the brothers, who were integral to his life and self, he'd depended on for survival and practical matters, never emotionally. He'd never felt he'd die if he lost them. He felt that about her, and more. He could live only with her.

This profound dependence had started from their first

meeting. Right then his fundamental being had recognized hers as the only one to mesh with it, to complete his missing parts. The feeling had taken root during the night he'd first claimed her, as she'd claimed him right back. Every day since, those roots had been growing deeper, becoming entangled, encompassing everything inside him.

Their intimacy, in and out of bed, had been growing exponentially, and she'd been totally open about what he made her feel. But she hadn't made a straight declaration of her love. He hadn't, either, but he had been calling her "my love" and "my heart" and "my soul" and meaning every word. She hadn't reciprocated.

But just before Richard arrived, something terrible had occurred to him. He couldn't believe it hadn't before. Being with her did tamper with his every mental function.

He'd realized he should hope she wouldn't declare her love. Not yet. Not before he settled his mission, and could tell her the whole truth…

"Seriously?" Richard's scoff yanked him out of his oppressive musings. "You're going to be one of those men who zones out when they even picture their beloved?"

He forced his focus back on Richard. "I said Jenan is off-limits. To discussion. To speculation. To thoughts."

"Thoughts, eh? You have a way of enforcing that ban?"

"If you value your family jewels, you'll shut up, give me that briefcase and get the hell out of here."

"Leave?" Richard feigned a shocked face. "Without taking a tour of this *Arabian Nights* reproduction?"

"I can take the briefcase from your dead body, Cobra."

Richard laughed, true amusement in the lethal rumble. "I'll die another day, thank you, Phantom." He swung the briefcase up, hugged it to his chest, provocation set on maximum. "I flew fifteen hours straight to come here. Doesn't this warrant that you offer me a drink, at least?"

"No, it doesn't. Now give me the damned documents."

"Just like that? I get nothing in return."

"You do. I owe you one. Collect it anytime."

"I'll collect it right now. I want that drink."

Numair seethed with frustration. He could always beat Richard to a pulp. Problem was, Richard would inflict as much damage on him. They were each other's match. And he couldn't have Jenan arriving to find him torn and bloody. His scars continued to hurt her, and he couldn't bear disturbing her anymore if he could help it. Which meant he couldn't vent his aggression. Ever again.

As he was about to take that insufferable creature to force-feed him that drink, Richard added, "And I want to meet that mythical being who brought you to your knees."

Numair rounded on him, snarling, "You can ask for anything of equal value to what you're giving me. *Anything* involving Jenan is invaluable, and will never be an option, for you or anyone else. But now you've dared to ask that, I wouldn't offer you a sip of water if you were dying of thirst, so you might as well give up and go the hell away."

Richard transferred the briefcase behind his back. "You know I never give up. And I'm going nowhere. So what will you do? Kill me like you've wanted to for the past twenty-five years?"

"If that's what it takes to get rid of you."

Richard's devil eyes flared with challenge, and Numair's body bunched in preparation for that climactic fight he'd been burning for since he'd been fifteen. But a deep sound doused his aggression.

The helicopter bringing Jenan to him.

As he relinquished his confrontation with Richard and rushed down the stairs to the helipad, Richard huffed a laugh.

"Saved by the copter." Numair turned his fed-up gaze to him, and Richard wiggled an eyebrow. "You were."

He stopped where he always waited for her, watching the helicopter landing, and Richard appeared beside him.

"I expect this is your beloved. What opportune timing. I'll get to meet her after all."

Suspicion exploded inside Numair's mind. "You timed your arrival so you'd intercept her."

Richard's eyebrows shot up in what looked like genuine incredulity. "Bloody hell, Phantom, you're in a far worse condition than I thought. How would I have known when she comes to visit? Or if she comes at fixed times at all?"

"You know anything you want to know."

"True. But that's only if I wanted to know. And a few minutes ago I didn't even realize that woman's significance to you. Why would I have tried to *intercept* her?"

That made sense to Numair. It was possible he was just being paranoid.

But he'd learned it always paid to be that and more. And with someone like Richard, nothing was ever at face value. Richard might have long realized his true feelings toward Jenan and was here to do some kind of mischief. He couldn't afford that. He had enough worries where she was concerned. He couldn't add a whiff of trouble to them. And Richard was trouble in its most concentrated form.

He grabbed Richard by his lapels, hauled him closer until their noses almost touched. "Listen, Cobra, if you think I was ever your enemy, it's nothing to what I'll be if you step a millimeter out of line. I'm indebted to you for acquiring the original signed documents releasing the last of Zafrana's stocks and bonds, but you're here only because you insisted they were too crucial to be entrusted to a messenger. I should have known you didn't come because you cared about the documents or my plans."

"No? If I don't care, why did I even help you in the first place? I could have just told you to sod off."

"Are you telling me you care now? If I live or die? This is you and me, Cobra, remember?"

Richard gave a gruff exhalation. "As if you ever let me forget. But I also remember we were once best friends."

"Yes, until you reported that I was planning to escape so you could gain your superiors' favor. My body still bears the scars of the sixty days straight they tortured me within an inch of my life in punishment."

There. He'd gotten it out in the open at last.

Richard stared at him for a long, charged moment. Then he exhaled. "Did you ever wonder why I did it?"

"No. Because I already knew why. You were a monster by choice and preference, Cobra. You still are."

After holding his eyes for another moment with an inexplicable expression filling his own, Richard finally shrugged. "As are you. Or at least, as you were, until Princess Aal Ghamdi."

Numair looked back as the helicopter landed, seething with urgency. "Don't think my feelings for her tame me, Cobra. A predator with a mate is even more deadly."

"But more vulnerable."

Before he could snarl a response, the copter's door was flung open and Jenan jumped out, hitting the ground running as usual. Forgetting Richard within a heartbeat, he swung around and rushed to meet her halfway.

Watching her run to him was, as always, an agonizing joy. Her hair caught the declining rays of the sun and reflected it into tones of fire and ruby. Her eyes rivaled its golden heat. Her smile was everything he lived to see anymore, her body everything he lived to feel and her whole being everything that embodied his reasons for existence.

Suddenly her expression sobered, and her steps faltered. Something sharp stabbed him in the gut at the loss of her eagerness, even when he realized it was on account of Richard's presence. She'd only just noticed that hulk. And it doused her spontaneity. Another thing for which to wish Richard an eternity in the deepest abyss.

As he covered the remaining distance and took her in his arms, Jenan asked, "Who is that?"

He gritted his teeth over the expletives on the tip of his tongue. "Richard Graves. My associate."

"Not one of your Black Castle brothers, is he?"

Numair's heart fired. Every time she mentioned his brothers or made a comment that correctly diagnosed a truth he hid, the need to tell her everything almost overpowered him. With those uncanny instincts of hers, she'd realized there was far more to him than what he'd made known.

But she accepted the darkest parts she knew of his manufactured history without reservations, with even admiration for what he'd become. It made him hope that when he was able to divulge the whole truth, it wouldn't shock her, wouldn't alienate her.

He now only said, "No, he's not."

"I thought Black Castle was exclusively a partnership between you and those men you consider brothers."

"Richard, regretfully, is the exception."

"Regretfully, huh?" She suddenly chuckled. "And he's still in one piece and living and unavoidably in your life, too? He is certainly a man worth meeting. Introduce me?"

Grinding his teeth again, he knew he had to comply. At least he'd made Richard realize he *would* kill him this time if he messed this up with Jenan. He hoped, for her sake, that Richard behaved. He'd rather not kill him in front of her.

Entwining her arm with his, he took her to meet Richard.

Deep into the night, Numair woke up with a start.

He subsided when he felt Jenan draped over him, every inch of her warm, firm, precious flesh plastered to his.

They'd made love for hours after Richard left. To his shock, Richard had behaved with perfect gallantry in Jenan's presence. And Jenan had been her usual spontaneous self with him. Numair, however, still wanted to kill him. He clearly had serious insecurity issues, even when he knew he had no reason to.

But he did have a reason, he corrected himself. A huge one. And it had nothing to do with jealousy.

During the past weeks, while everything had fallen into place according to his methodical plans, with him releasing Jenan from Hassan, then forcing him to relinquish Zafrana's debts one at a time, with the last ones being what Richard had brought him today, he'd kept realizing that nothing was going as he'd envisioned.

The cousins he'd come here intending to engage in a vicious fight were nothing he'd thought they were. They were all admirable men and women. Even worse, he liked Najeeb more every time he saw him. His plan to wrest the throne from him after condemning his father for a murderer and destroying his family honor no longer seemed feasible. For how could he deal with Najeeb with as much cold blood as he'd always dealt with adversaries when he no longer considered him one?

But that was only his secondary worry. His main one was focused on Jenan. The foreboding that had been building inside him had crystallized during Richard's visit.

At first, he hadn't thought a day would come when he'd regret not being honest about why he'd wanted an heir.

But if he put the rest of his plan into action, she'd realize his early purpose. He had no doubt the totally honest woman that she was, who'd accepted his declared reasons in good faith, would feel betrayed and used. Now he didn't know how to rectify his initial mistake.

His only hope was that she wasn't already pregnant.

Which was probably too much to hope for after their weeks of unprotected lovemaking.

But she must have been checking regularly, and if she'd said nothing, it was possible she wasn't yet pregnant. If she wasn't, he didn't want her to get pregnant anymore. He didn't want a child to complicate matters between them more than they already were, to make her more prone to being vulnerable and inconsolable when the truth came out.

But he wouldn't know where to go from here until he asked her, knew for certain if she was or wasn't pregnant.

Coming to that conclusion, he closed his eyes again and did something he'd never done before.

He prayed. To whatever was out there and might listen. He prayed that she wasn't pregnant, that he'd be granted a second chance to make this right.

Jen watched Numair prowling toward her in the mirror as she brushed her hair in long, leisurely strokes, imagining herself stroking his magnificent body.

Not that she needed imagining. He'd given her absolute freedom to do whatever she wished to him and she'd been losing her mind all over him, doing everything she'd ever dreamed of with that body of his. And he'd been doing everything she'd known about, and many, many things she hadn't known about, with hers. To both their complete and supreme ecstasy.

He now came to tower over her from behind, his eyes flaring and subsiding like glowing emeralds, snaring her eyes in their reflection. In her mind she only saw a sequence of events that had happened so many times during the past six delirious weeks. Numair picking her up, making her feel weightless, thrilling her yet again with all the power this man of hers possessed. And how he used it all to worship and pleasure her!

Then his hands descended on her shoulders, and she

shuddered in anticipation, though she knew she shouldn't be inviting another session of passion. She'd told her father she'd be back in the palace in an hour to give him proof Zafrana's debts, and his mess, had been wiped clean. Thanks to Numair.

But surely her father could wait a few hours longer…

"Have you…checked?"

Numair's quiet question felt like a slap of icy water across her heated body and fantasies.

There wasn't any use wondering what he was asking about. His meaning was totally clear. And her instant mortification had an equally known origin.

For she hadn't checked.

She'd been avoiding doing so. She hadn't wanted to make sure if she was pregnant, even now that her period was late. He might have insisted that wanting her had come first, and still did, but she feared that becoming pregnant would destroy their intimacy, not solidify it.

She also believed he'd insisted on marriage early on in order to give his heir the legitimacy she now suspected he'd never had. He'd always avoided talking much about his past, but she was now convinced the facts he made known were nothing but a fabrication, that he'd never had a family, and that his childhood had been too terrible to share.

She wanted to do anything at all to make it up to him, to give him everything he wanted and needed, yet she couldn't bear that he'd marry her for any other reason but for her.

And there was another concern. Though he'd been deluging her in his passion and consideration, she still felt him holding back…*so* much. Not knowing what he was hiding of himself, of his past, she couldn't chart the future.

That was why she dreaded changing the present. And her pregnancy would blow that up big-time.

Instead of saying she hadn't checked, she said, "There's nothing yet."

And it was as if a dagger drove into her heart.

That flare in his eyes. That convulsive squeeze of her shoulders. That shudder that emanated from his body and reverberated in her own.

He was *relieved*.

That she *wasn't* pregnant.

The magnitude of his relief had almost rocked him off his feet. If he hadn't grabbed her shoulders so hard, she thought he might have even slumped to his knees.

His reaction was so startling, so incongruous with everything she'd believed up till this point, about him and about what he wanted. She felt beyond shocked.

And there was only one explanation she could find.

He'd changed his mind.

He no longer wanted to have an heir.

Not from her.

Numair didn't know how it was possible, after all he'd done in his life, that he'd deserved a second chance.

Yet he'd somehow gotten it.

Jenan wasn't pregnant yet.

The news had almost buckled his knees when bullets had failed to do so. Relief still so enervated him, he hadn't been able to do anything since she'd left for Zafrana's royal palace an hour ago.

This development bought him the most precious commodity—time to resolve everything. This way he could let it be her choice to give him a child after she knew everything about him, and everything that had brought him into her life. He wanted nothing but for her to have the dignity, the freedom and self-determination to decide to be with him, to share her life and child with him, after full disclosure.

This was everything he wanted now. He no longer cared about taking over Zafrana's throne or even Saraya's. He no longer even cared about punishing his uncle or avenging his father or himself. All the ugliness and horrors and suffering suddenly felt as though they had happened in someone else's past, someone he no longer was.

He was now a new man, a man who loved Jenan with all the heart she'd created inside him. He cared only that she forgave him his initial deception and gave him her trust, her love, forever. Nothing else but her mattered.

As for resolving the other matters he'd come here for, his plans had radically changed. He still had to depose Hassan, as this was no longer just about him, but because he couldn't let such a criminal continue ruling his homeland. He now just had to find a way that wouldn't hurt or disgrace the rest of Hassan's family…and his own. Then he'd be able to confess everything to Jenan.

Suddenly, another realization burst in his mind.

He couldn't make love to her anymore!

Though there was a possibility he couldn't impregnate her since he hadn't yet—which he also realized didn't matter at all—he couldn't continue making love to her without protection, in case they finally succeeded in creating a child before he resolved everything. And he couldn't suddenly start using protection, either, not without explaining why.

His only way out was to not make love to her at all. It felt like the most mutilating sentence he'd ever had inflicted on him. But it was a price he had to pay for his mistakes, until he fixed them and told her the truth.

He could only pray to whoever or whatever had answered his first prayer, that when he did, she'd still want him and would give him a second chance.

The second chance his life depended on.

"Is Numair coming today?"

At Fayza's eager question, Jen turned from staring

numbly at her reflection in her bedroom mirror. She found both her sisters with their heads poking around her suite's door, their long hair cascading like waterfalls of mahogany and ebony. They were now the one thing that made being back in Zafrana's royal palace, in Zafrana at all, in this whole life, bearable.

She had one response for them. "No, he isn't coming."

And she feared he never would again.

"But we want to ask him if we can have another party on board his jet," Zeena lamented.

"Can we call him?" Fayza zoomed inside, bombarding her with questions. "We don't have his phone number. Does he even answer if it's a number he doesn't know? Or does he know our numbers? Would you call him for us?"

"Don't you think we've taken enough from Sheikh Numair?"

Jen's heart squeezed at their father's weary voice. He now followed the girls into her suite at a much slower pace, as if it hurt to walk.

Forcing a smile, she rose to greet him, and he took her in arms that trembled and kissed the top of her head.

It felt as if her father had grown smaller in the past months, had aged far beyond his sixty-three years. Being helpless to solve his kingdom's problems, and the shame of having to sacrifice his eldest daughter as their only solution had taken their toll. Even now that it was over, it seemed the ordeal still echoed its distress and defeat inside him. It probably would for the rest of his life.

She pulled back, wanting to soothe him, even when she had nothing but dread and pain inside her own soul, and he looked at her with a world of contrition in his eyes.

"When you first came to me with Numair and told me he'd resolve Zafrana's debts, I couldn't believe he'd do that without asking for something even bigger in return. I didn't even know if he could do it. Then Hassan called everything off, and I knew Numair had fulfilled his promise. A week ago, I got back everything I signed away, just because Numair willed it. Now I find myself in an even bigger debt than what bound me in servitude to Hassan. This time to Numair. The debt of the restoration of your freedom, of our kingdom's stability and of my dignity. And it's a debt I have no idea how I will ever repay."

Swallowing the knot in her throat, she tried to keep the tremors of anguish from her voice. "Numair doesn't want, or expect, anything in return."

Numair didn't want anything anymore. Not from her.

"Are you certain, *ya b'nayti*?" She winced at how her father called her "my daughter," as his eyes, so much like hers, probed her in hope. "I thought you were the prize he had his heart set on."

Unable to utter another word without succumbing to the desolate weeping that had overcome her so many times in the past week, she just shook her head.

That hit her family hard, made them cut their visit short. They'd all come with everything they'd wanted to say or hoped for involving Numair. They'd had their hearts set on Numair ending up with her.

As she'd believed he would. Until that day she'd told him she wasn't pregnant.

Since that day, he'd been finding excuses not to meet her, and if he had to, he made sure it wasn't in their place or anywhere private. Every instance of pointed distance had solidified her suspicions. He *had* been relieved she hadn't become pregnant, and he wasn't risking she might become so. But it was far worse than she'd at first thought. It wasn't the heir he'd changed his mind about.

It was her. He no longer wanted her.

It had taken her seven weeks to fall irrevocably in love with him, to become unable to think how she'd lived before him, or to imagine a life without him. It had taken him the same time to have enough of her.

Who was she fooling? It hadn't taken her that long to fall for him. She'd done so on sight. Every day since had only driven her deeper into dependence.

And while his desire for her had seemed to intensify, too, it had just come to an abrupt end that day. Ever since, he'd been pretending to still want her, but he escaped any intimacy under a dozen pretexts. He might think he was letting her down gradually, but she couldn't bear that. If he no longer wanted her, she wanted it over. Now.

Waga'a sa'aa wala kol sa'aa. The pain of an hour rather than that of every hour.

The adage was true. But she knew this pain would only grow until it consumed her. For this was worse than anything she'd feared. Just before her family had come, she'd succumbed and…checked. The two pink lines had appeared instantaneously. It was as she'd feared for some time now.

She *was* pregnant.

Knowing for sure that she carried the baby of the only man she could ever love—when he no longer wanted that child or her—was pure, unremitting agony.

Now she wanted, *needed*, to look him in the eye and get the closure of hearing him say it.

That he no longer wanted a child. Or her. That he'd never really wanted her, not as she wanted him.

That it was over.

Nine

Numair stood aside and let Najeeb pass inside what he and Jenan had come to call *Malaz*, or Sanctuary. Their home.

The home he'd contrived not to let her come to for a whole week now. He'd known if she came, he'd succumb to his need, and more, to hers. The questions, the uncertainty in her eyes every time he'd seen her at the palace or elsewhere with others around during the past week had been killing him. But he hoped, after Najeeb's visit, the separation he'd enforced on them would be over forever.

He'd invited Najeeb here to face him with the truth.

Najeeb regarded him with confusion as Numair invited him to sit down where he had the first time he'd come here. Their relationship had changed radically over the past weeks since that hostile first meeting. But their interactions had remained with Jenan at their core. No doubt Najeeb couldn't understand what they had to discuss in her absence.

Najeeb asked at once, "Is this about Jenan?"

Numair sat down on the armchair facing him. "Everything is ultimately about Jenan. But this is about you. And me. And our family."

Najeeb went still, his face freezing. "*Our* family?"

"Yes." He leaned forward, pushed toward him the dossier with all the evidence of his identity.

The teams he'd had scouring the Mediterranean with Black Castle patented equipment and technology had found the sunken yacht. And the remains. A DNA test had proved his memories without a doubt. The remains were incontrovertibly of Hisham Aal Ghaanem. Hassan's brother. And Numair's father.

Najeeb went through each document, mounting shock an expanding sweep emanating from him.

Then Najeeb raised his eyes, and there was something there that shocked Numair in turn. The last thing he'd expected Najeeb to feel. Delight.

"You're my cousin!"

Numair's throat closed. Najeeb's reaction rocked him to his core. He'd been bracing for Najeeb's disbelief, suspicion, dismay and a dozen other things that would be natural reactions when faced with a revelation of this magnitude. But this—the unmistakable acceptance and instant eagerness—hadn't even been reactions he'd imagined. Najeeb continued to decimate his every expectation. And if he'd already been wondering how to become his antagonist and rival for the throne, he now wondered if he could be.

Najeeb sat forward, every line in his body explicit with his excitement. "*Ya Ullah*, after all these years! What happened? How did you find out? Did you just find out? *B'Ellahi*, this is incredible, amazing! Wait till Haroon and Jawad and my other siblings find out about this! The girls especially will go ballistic. They've been swooning over you, and now they'll have premium bragging rights. But we'll have to make it clear right off the bat to every other lady in our family and acquaintance that you're the exclusive property of Jenan—"

Hating to do it, Numair had to interrupt his zeal. "I got you in private because I don't want anyone but you to know. You'll realize why when I tell you the whole story."

Numair couldn't believe how it dismayed him to see the spontaneity in the other man's eyes dimming. He'd no doubt extinguish it completely if he declared his right to the throne.

For now, he told him the story he'd already decided to tell him. The attack, his father's murder and how he'd been left for dead, and the fictional parts about being rescued then adopted, then back to the truth of retrieving his memories of the incident after years of hypnotherapy.

Najeeb looked more moved with every word. Then he let out a ragged exhalation. "But this means you knew your true identity when we first met. Why didn't you tell me then?"

"Because I was still searching for the proof you have in your hands now."

"You thought I wouldn't believe you without evidence?" Najeeb seemed stunned that Numair had considered such a thing.

"Wouldn't you?"

"To borrow your and Jenan's favorite catchphrase, you're kidding, right? After my initial hostility, which was all concern for Jenan, I felt a kindred link to you that I couldn't explain. I would have believed you without any proof beyond those of my instincts." Suddenly, he laughed. "But it's your lady's instincts that are uncanny. She's the one who saw through it all from the first moment, who kept saying we felt as close as brothers. As we are."

"As we are," Numair repeated, something hot and overriding stirring in his chest.

He had his brothers, and they were an essential part of his being. But the tug of blood between him and Najeeb was something he'd never experienced, or expected to. Since the last trace of worry he could rival him for Jenan's affection had been erased, and now that Najeeb accepted him so readily, he let it sweep him.

He hated to spoil those moments of closeness, to tarnish the purity of Najeeb's goodwill. But he had to tell him the rest.

"Making contact with my long-lost family wasn't why I went to your father's reception. Or why I came here."

That again stunned Najeeb. "What else did you want?"

"To reclaim my birthright. And to exact vengeance."

The light in Najeeb's eyes went out. "Vengeance?"

"I believed your father had mine killed."

To say Najeeb was shocked was like saying Numair slightly liked Jenan. Numair could feel his statement tearing through the other man's very foundations.

Then shock gave way to adamant rejection, and Najeeb just said, "No."

Before Numair could respond, a sound emptied his mind. That of the helicopter that had been bringing him Jenan for the past weeks. All but this last one.

He heaved up to his feet. "We'll discuss this at length, Najeeb. But for now just stay here and wait for me."

Before Najeeb could even blink, Numair ran out.

He had no idea how he'd send Jenan away without explaining why, but he couldn't have her see Najeeb. The can of worms had been opened, but nothing had yet been resolved.

By the time he crossed the villa, she was already opening the front door. He rushed to intercept her, and she raised her gaze to him. What he saw in her eyes made him almost stumble.

She looked…bereft.

Forcing his legs to work, he reached her as she closed the door, and pulled her into his arms. "Is everyone all right?"

She nodded, but pushed out of his arms when she always clung.

At a loss what to make of her disturbing disposition, he said, "You didn't tell me you were coming."

Her eyes again rose to his, and they looked so wounded, foreboding pierced his heart. "You would have only found a way to escape seeing me. But don't worry, I won't stay where I'm no longer welcome."

He gaped at her. "What?"

"You should have told me the truth the moment you realized it."

Everything inside him stilled. Had she somehow found out the truth and it was too late to be the one to tell her? Was that the reaction he'd been dreading?

He finally choked out, "What truth?"

"That you no longer want me."

This was literally the last thing he'd expected her to say. It hit him so hard, everything in his mind fractured.

"Jenan, this is insane…"

"Yes, it seems my name is quite apt. I must be insane to feel crushed now when you already told me what you wanted from the get-go. But you don't want it from me anymore, and I'm here to tell you it's your right to change your mind. But it isn't your right to drag this out, to not just release me. If you think evading me is letting me down easy, it's far more painful than if you'd just looked me in the eye and told me it's over."

Every word fell on him like a sledgehammer.

He'd been so consumed in his worries and efforts to put things right, he'd made things catastrophically worse. He hadn't even thought how his evasions would seem to her, but she'd found them so inexplicable, so hurtful, she'd reached the worst possible conclusion.

Before he could think of anything to say, she strode past him, heading toward where Najeeb was seated.

He pounced to stop her. "Where are you going?"

The spasm of pain that twisted her face almost tore his heart apart. "I said not to worry. I won't try to stay or to impose on you. I'll just get some stuff I need. You can send the rest later. Or just throw it away."

He wanted to blurt out a thousand protests, but only one thing made it out of the churning mess in his mind. "This is *your* place."

Her forlorn expression deepened, widening the wound her pain had gouged in his being. "I only considered it mine when I thought you were, too, when we were together. But you're not, and we won't be again. Tomorrow I'll send you the papers reverting the ownership to you." She tried to move again, and his hand tightened convulsively on her arm with horror at the terrible things she believed. And suspicion blossomed like an ink stain in her eyes. "You have someone inside?"

Shocked all over again at her horrific assumption, more evidence of how disastrously he'd messed up, he could only stare at her helplessly.

And everything in her eyes died. It felt far worse than anything he'd endured in captivity, seeing that look in her eyes.

"Jenan, please…"

Tears arrowed down her cheeks, drowning her words and his. "I never expected you to love me as I loved you. I only ever wanted you to be honest with me."

Hearing her for the first time say she loved him—only for her to make it in the past tense—was unbearable. Like knowing he could have saved someone's life, and out of his own negligence, he'd arrived just moments too late.

This time he didn't let her resist him, but crushed her in his arms. "Jenan, Jenan, what have I done to you, to us? I damaged your trust in me so much you think I have a woman in there?" A tear splashed over his chest, corroding its way through to his heart as she shook all over and struggled to escape his embrace. He crushed her to him harder, groaned between feverish kisses all over her face. "Everything you think is the absolute opposite of the truth. It agonizes me to know I made you think it. But it's true I don't love you like you love me." At her lurching sob, he squeezed her tighter, as if he'd merge her into his body. "After all I've suffered in my life, I love you far more than you can ever love me."

This time when she struggled, it was to look up.

Her eyes looked so fragile and inflamed she had to have been weeping long before she'd come. But that dreadful grief was giving way to hope. His heart swelled with impending relief only to shrivel the next second.

"It's true he doesn't have a woman in there. The secrets he's been hiding are far, far worse than that."

Both he and Jenan swung around at the dark drawl.

Numair's arms loosened around Jenan with dismay, letting her go as her face went slack with surprise. "Najeeb."

He couldn't have them both here now. It might cause a chain reaction he wouldn't be able to control.

Numair turned urgently to Jenan. "I do have secrets, but they have nothing to do with us, with what I feel for you. I also have reasons for the way I've been behaving, and I'll explain everything, only later. Please, *ya habibati*, just go now, let me conclude this with Najeeb and trust that everything I do is for you, for us."

As Jenan's eyes softened with such relief and tension left her body, Najeeb's harsh sarcasm washed over them once more, stiffening her all over again.

"Your powers of manipulation border on magic, don't

they, Numair?" Najeeb's steps were measured, his face as hard as stone, his eyes simmering with rage. Then he turned his gaze to Jenan. "When I heard your anguish as I approached, I thought he'd told you everything." His gaze swung back to Numair. "But then I realized you were still playing her. What I felt the moment I saw you *was* right. There are far darker things to you, and colder, more terrible motives to your being with her than even I feared. But you realized I was on to you, and you poured on the pretense, conned me like you conned her from the start."

"I might have hidden some truths—"

"Some truths?" Najeeb scoffed. "You hid every truth. All the time we've been dealing with a total fabrication."

"This *is* the real me. I only had to settle things with you first before I told her everything."

"About that." Najeeb flicked him a contemptuous look. "I sat in there wondering why you revealed your truth now, and I realized it's because you've reached the point in your meticulous plans when it suited you to do so, when you were ready to strike. But when you looked so shaken by Jenan's arrival, and so anxiously asked me to stay inside, I realized this was one thing you didn't account for. For us to meet at this delicate point, exposing everything to her prematurely. According to your plans, she would have been the last to know the truth, right? When it was too late for her to do anything about it."

Unable to act on his rising dread and aggression, Numair said, "You have this all wrong, Najeeb."

Until this moment, Jenan had been mutely gaping at them. Now she came between them, her voice a brittle tremolo. "What plans? What truth?"

Before Numair could try to mollify her again, Najeeb ended any hope for containing this disaster.

"That his name isn't Numair, but ironically, a synonym

of that, what I'm sure he meant. It's Fahad. Fahad Aal Ghaanem."

After seconds of nonreaction, the widening of Jenan's eyes said that she recognized the name. The confusion that flooded them right after said she couldn't process, or believe, the connotations of that name.

Najeeb ended her uncertainty. "Yes, *that* Fahad Aal Ghaanem. The cousin we all thought long dead."

It took frozen moments before Jenan shook her head, her bewilderment deepening, not lessening. "How?"

In answer, Najeeb succinctly recounted the story he'd told him. As he spoke, Jenan's eyes were riveted to Numair, as if struggling to superimpose the new truths on what she'd known of him, what she'd had with him, till now.

When Najeeb fell silent, she asked shakily, "Why didn't you tell me?"

It was Najeeb who answered again. "This was another thing I sat in there trying to understand. Then I worked it all out. You see, right before you arrived, Numair—or should I say Fahad—told me he was here to exact revenge. On my father, whom he accused of having his father killed. The other reason he mentioned was to reclaim his *birthright*. And it all became clear. He had a convoluted plan to come here, hurt my father as much as possible until he had solid proof of his lineage. Once he did, he'd accuse my father of murder, deposing him in a scandal and of course getting rid of me as the current crown prince, and claiming the throne for himself." Najeeb turned to Numair, arctic challenge in those eyes that had been all warmth such a short while ago. "Did I miss anything?"

"It's not like that anymore…"

"What about me?"

Jenan's voice, so smothered in trepidation, drove a jagged edge in his gut, cutting short his protestations.

"Jenan, I said I'll explain everything later…"

"Will you?" Najeeb's words cut through his entreaty like a knife. "Why not do it now? She's asking a very simple question after all. Why did you approach her in the first place? Or should we say, target her? That was the other thing I sat in there trying to figure out, until I finally realized that your *heritage* isn't only in Saraya, but Zafrana. Your mother was Princess Safeyah Aal Ghamdi, and half of your blood is royal Zafranian blood. Being the power-monger that you are, and with the state the kingdom is in, you must consider you're the one who has both the right and the power to rule it. But since you don't have a direct claim to the throne as you do in Saraya, you concocted a more convoluted plan. You weren't *saving* Jenan from my father, or even trying to hurt him by decimating his power over Zafrana and the massive resources he'd expended to gain it. You wanted Jenan only to use her in the exact same way he intended to." Najeeb turned his pained gaze to Jenan. "Claiming you, having an heir from you, would make him control Zafrana's throne during your father's life, then after his death, until his heir, your father's heir, comes of age."

Jenan turned her gaze toward Numair. There was no shock or pain or accusation in there. Just emptiness.

As everything collided inside him, the vacuum in her eyes intensified, as if her essence had totally departed his body. A body that had nothing more to prop it up, and collapsed to the ground in a boneless mass.

"Jenan!"

Lightning-fast reflexes honed through decades of merciless training kicked in, fighting off the paralysis. He caught her before she hit the ground. But Najeeb had also charged to save her.

Finding Najeeb's hands crowding his on Jenan's inert body almost made his head burst with rage.

As soon as he laid her down with trembling care on the ground, he flung Najeeb away and tackled him there.

Najeeb was so stunned by his attack, Numair got a few jaw-cracking punches in before Najeeb pulled himself together enough to retaliate. At the first blow that connected with Numair's own jaw, something crashed in place inside him, rousing him from his blind wrath.

Najeeb was a powerful man, could hold his own with anyone else, but he wasn't a violent man, and certainly not a killer. But Numair was. Najeeb was no match for him. If he didn't curb himself, he would kill him.

Flinging himself off him and rebounding to his feet, he watched Najeeb rise to his, rubbing his already swelling jaw as if to make sure it was still hinged. Numair *had* pulled his punches, or it would have been pulverized now.

Looking at him as if at a horrific monster, Najeeb rasped with obvious difficulty, "What *are* you?"

"Something you can't even imagine in your worst nightmares. Consider yourself lucky. I have destroyed men for causing me far, far less than the incalculable damage you just caused me with Jenan."

As Numair moved, Najeeb's body stiffened in readiness for confrontation. "Stay where you are, you maniac."

Numair shot him a baleful glance as he rushed back to Jenan, scooped her unconscious form up and took her to their bed, where he'd missed having her like he'd miss a vital organ. She was warm, breathing easily. It seemed her nervous system had sought the refuge of oblivion to protect her from the brunt of Najeeb's revelations.

After minutes of trying to rouse her and failing, but knowing she was in no danger, he rose and turned to Najeeb, who'd followed him, as if not trusting him with Jenan now.

"I'm over my murderous fury, which thanks to your punch—" he rubbed his own jaw; Najeeb's punch would have felled any other man "—I realized was directed at myself. You only exposed the truth about what I once intended."

Najeeb tried a bitter laugh, and it came out a pained groan. "You know where you went wrong? If you'd come clean to me, to Jenan, if you weren't a cold, manipulative bastard, we would have gladly given you everything you wanted. I would have recognized your right to the throne, would have made my father relinquish it to you." He nodded toward Jenan. "And she would have loved you. Of her own free will, and would have considered you the one who deserves Zafrana's throne. Now I wouldn't entrust the fate of a heap of dirt to you, let alone that of my kingdom. And if you spread your vicious lies about my father and try to destroy my family, I'll fight you till my dying breath. As for her, don't hold *your* breath you'll be able to con her again."

Numair exhaled. "Though you might not believe it now, I got you here so I can resolve this with minimum damage to everyone. But you didn't let me finish what I had to say, and now anything you think is irrelevant. Fixing things with you will have to wait until I deal with this disaster you've caused me with Jenan."

Najeeb's antipathy wavered, before his gaze panned to Jenan and it turned to steel again. "You can try. But this woman would have died for you. If I know anything about her, she'd now rather die than let you near her again."

Turning to Najeeb fully, he let him see the monster he had inside him, and that he could no longer harness it. "You better pray that your prediction doesn't come to pass. If I lose her, I will have nothing else to lose in this world. Not even I can predict what I'd do then."

Najeeb must have realized it was dangerous to continue antagonizing him, and was clearly uncertain if he even should, because with a last glance full of confusion, he turned and walked out.

He fell off Numair's radar at once as he swooped down to Jenan, wrapping himself around her.

He wasn't losing her. Najeeb underestimated the power of what they had. She'd listen to him, and she'd understand, and she'd believe him again, trust him again.

Love him again.

Something hot and hard spread over Jenan, as smothering and inescapable as a shroud of burning steel.

Panic flooded her as she started to struggle, even when she knew there could be no escape. Sobs tore from her depths, gurgled to the surface.

"Shh, shh, *ya hayati*, calm down, everything is all right, you're safe. I'm here, and I'm yours."

That voice… Numair's voice. It had been the one thing she wanted to hear, the one thing to make her feel invincible. But now it made her suffocate with betrayal and misery.

The surge of memories tore her from the abyss she'd plummeted into and catapulted her into the far more horrible reality.

But she couldn't hide within oblivion anymore. She had to open her eyes and face him. Face the fact that her life would be nothing like she'd hoped or planned, but rather like everything she'd dreaded in other women's lives. Having the child of a man who cared nothing for her, suffering the perpetual heartaches and conflicts of being tied to him through that child for life.

But it was even worse in her condition. For even after finding out the truth, she knew she'd never stop yearning for him. For the Numair she'd loved. The Numair who didn't exist.

She opened her eyes and found him there, like dozens

of times before, wrapped around her, looking down at her as if only she mattered to him. When she now knew she never did at all.

"He's no longer here."

If desolation had a sound, this had to be it. The bleeding whisper that issued from her.

He blinked. "Yes, Najeeb left…"

"Numair." When she said his name, he sat up carefully, uncertain what she meant. She left him in doubt. "He was never here. He was a phantom."

He started at her description, looked stricken. "Jenan…"

She spoke over his ragged protest. "Everything I shared with him was a lie." She looked him in the eyes, and it almost ruptured her heart that they still looked like those of the Numair she adored, still uncannily hid the true nature of the malicious manipulator she now knew him to be. "I was a means to your ends. A chess piece you used and would have sacrificed as soon as you achieved your goal. But when you discovered you could do so now rather than later, you just cut me off."

His fingers sank into her shoulders, his eyes raging like infernos. "Don't even think that. None of that is true. Let me explain what Najeeb—"

"Najeeb only told me who you really are." She removed his hands from her flesh and pulled herself away from him. "I worked out the rest. For Najeeb doesn't know what I do. That you no longer have to marry me, or impregnate me to rule Zafrana, that you do have a direct claim to its throne, just like you do to Saraya's."

The need became desperation to escape the distress of his nearness and of being in the bed where he'd given her her life's only true and total pleasures, and then ruined her for life. She rose as if she'd been smashed and put back together with a precarious glue.

As he rose after her, she went on, "It's no wonder it took

you a while to find out. It was almost four decades ago, and most people in Zafrana don't know about it. Those who do probably don't remember it."

"Remember what? Jenan, *habibati*, just let me—"

"But I remember." Her choking whisper again silenced him. "How my father always lamented that he shouldn't have been king, that if not for a fluke accident, he wouldn't have been the rightful heir. He told me so many times when I was growing up that the late King Zayd had an heir who was tragically lost as an infant. The son of Princess Safeyah, a distant relative to the king by blood, but his sister in nursing, his mother having nursed her when her mother died in childbirth. This relationship superseded the much closer link of blood between him and my father, making her son his closest male relative, and his heir. You."

Silence and stillness expanded at her back as his surprise buffeted her. He hadn't realized that she knew.

But she did. And it explained all her questions about him, her incredulities about his coming into her life and her confusions about his recent turnabout.

Suddenly, his hands fell on her shoulders, feeling like twin bolts of torment that almost reduced her to ashes, his groan ragged. "Jenan, you have to believe me, I didn't know that."

She tore his hands off before they burned her through to the bone, then turned on him. "You didn't know that until you wasted too much time on me. But the moment you did, you tossed me aside." Another suspicion hit her, becoming a new terrible reality within a heartbeat. "But if you're trying to coax me again now, it means you know."

"I'm only trying to tell you the truth. I didn't know any of what you just said. And—" He suddenly stopped as her last words registered. Then he rasped, "Know what?"

"That I'm pregnant."

His instantaneous reaction was one of such consternation, it felt as if the heart hanging inside her by tattered strings was torn out completely and hurled on the ground.

The storm of misery that had been building inside her for the past week broke over her like a hurricane, destroying her soul and sanity.

She wept so hard, her tears became a downpour, draining her of everything that powered her being. Her hopes, her faith, her love…her soul.

She writhed weakly in his arms as he groaned and begged and tried to contain her in the now-oppressive circle of his arms, the embrace of deceit and cruelty.

Sobs hacked her insides and her words. "Now you know…your heir exists…you want to have it with the least conflict with the one who's regretfully carrying it…and what better way…than to con me again? The stupid, trusting, lovesick mark…you played from the first moment."

"No, Jenan, no, you have to listen to me."

"No…you listen. I loved Numair…I would have died for him, but now it's worse than if I'd simply lost him. Now I know that he never existed."

"I not only exist, and would die for you, but I only came fully into existence when I loved you. Before you, I never truly lived… Jenan, *habibati*, believe me…"

Unable to bear the scorching agony of his touch, she fought him frantically until he let her go.

She ended up against the door, sobs stabbing in her chest like skewers. He towered over her, a tempest of frustration and agitation raging on his face, knotting his every muscle. No doubt because things were no longer going his way.

But as everything in her clamored for him—the man who'd been as close to her as her very heart—another wave of desolation crashed on her. For she now knew.

She'd never rid her essence of the need for him. She'd never drain the poison of yearning from her blood without draining her very life with it. She'd never truly live again. Instead, she was doomed to just survive. For others. And without the man she'd loved, the man who'd turned out to be an illusion.

Once the conviction struck her, her weeping turned off abruptly. The suffering and desperation were too vast for tears. All that was left to feel was the resignation.

A deadened rasp issued from a throat that felt cut by thorns. "If you'd told me the truth, I would have realized you were the one powerful enough to save Zafrana. And if you'd wanted me at all, for real, I would have taken what I could with you even knowing you'd never feel for me what I feel for you. When you got enough of me, I would have at least remained intact. You could have gotten everything you wanted without destroying me."

She opened the door and spilled outside. Finding the helicopter still there was like finding a means of escape out of a flooding tunnel.

Before she stumbled to her salvation, he caught her back, his entreaties incessant.

Unable to endure one more touch or word, she wrenched herself from his arms with the last of her strength. "Don't you get it? You don't need to act anymore. I'm the one who's at your nonexistent mercy, who'll beg you not to deprive me of my baby. You won. Your plans worked. You'll have everything. Everything but me. But that won't matter to you, since I'm the only thing you never wanted."

Ten

So this was helplessness. This was desperation.

After a life of unimaginable ordeals, Numair had finally learned what these were. He'd been abused in every way, tortured to within a breath of his life, and he hadn't known anything like the sanity-destroying dread of the letdown, the desolation, the *end*, in Jenan's eyes.

And he couldn't do anything about it. Still, every cell in his body now fused with the manic urge to rampage after her, bring her back and keep her prisoner until he made her listen, made her believe him again.

But his every attempt to pull her away from the edge had only hurled her deeper into the abyss of distrust and betrayal. Anything more would only make things worse. She was in shock, and it would only intensify before it lessened. He had no idea when she'd be ready to listen to him. If she ever would again.

Suddenly, the sound of a helicopter approaching almost

made his heart detonate with hope. He found himself outside without even realizing he'd moved.

Then everything inside him shriveled again.

It wasn't her. It was Najeeb.

He stood there as the helicopter landed, as Najeeb jumped off, and hoped the man wasn't back to antagonize him again. He couldn't trust himself to pull back this time.

The signs of his earlier attack were becoming more evident by the second in the swelling and discoloration of Najeeb's face. But there was something new in the depths of his eyes. Not the early antipathy or the fleeting warmth or the recent bitterness. He looked troubled, anxious.

Najeeb started talking before he stopped before Numair. "When you said that my father had yours murdered, was that what you intended to say to shove both him and me from your path to the throne, or is it what you really believe?"

Needing to get rid of him fast, Numair gave him the short version of the truth. "It is what I believe."

"And you still got me here to seek a resolution?"

Najeeb answered his nod with a curt one, as if he now believed him. "Will you give me a chance to investigate this? I can't even begin to consider that my father is capable of such a crime."

He shook his head. "Listen, Najeeb—"

"No, you listen." Najeeb's agitation was no longer aggressive but entreating. "I'm not proud of my father. I know he's vain, imprudent and sometimes unethical, but I *know* him. He's not evil. And it would have taken unimaginable evil to have his own brother killed for the sake of the throne. He might appear power hungry, but he isn't. He's just a proud man who found himself in a role much larger than himself. He's done a decent job considering he inherited the kingdom in terrible shape from my grandfather. But unable to do better, and not having the best counselors, he turned to expansion to sustain the kingdom, like his bid to reannex Jareer, and once that failed, turning to Zafrana.

"But he never wanted the throne. Everyone who was around at the time would tell you how distraught he was after his brother's disappearance, how obsessively he searched for him, that even after being forced to abandon the search, he wouldn't sit on the throne until a year later, and didn't attempt to rule for yet another year, hoping his brother would return. But his cabinet eventually shamed and provoked him into taking his unexpected role seriously, and here we are today. Saraya, even with my father's mistakes, is a better kingdom than the one he'd inherited."

He ran a trembling hand over his close-cropped hair and blew out a heavy breath. "But not only am I convinced he isn't capable of having anyone murdered, let alone the older brother he worshipped, I'm also certain he would step down once he realizes who you are. In fact, he might even be relieved to finally relinquish the throne to its true heir."

Numair stared at Najeeb as he fell silent. He had heard everything Najeeb had said, but there was nothing inside him but the need to go after Jenan. Still, he had to say something to Najeeb.

All that came out when he opened his mouth was "I'm sorry I hit you, Najeeb."

Najeeb waved away his apology. "I was halfway back to Saraya when I realized no matter how you started with Jenan, you now truly love her. And that I caused a major breach between you and deserved a few broken bones— what I realize you could have easily given me, not just this lockjaw and black eyes in progress."

Needing this over now, Numair said, "I'm the one who gave Jenan every reason to suspect me. And I now believe Saraya's true heir is you. You're the one who lived there most of your life, who knows the country, who the people believe in and love. You're also the one who ameliorated your father's mistakes. Whatever Saraya is today, it's because of you, not him. But all this has nothing to do with what I believe about your father."

After a moment of total surprise, Najeeb's wariness was back full force. "So you still believe he had your father killed and you will still expose him?"

"No. I can't do that to you or to your siblings. This was what I got you here to tell you. That I'll force him to step down so you can take his place, not me."

This seemed to horrify Najeeb. "*B'Ellahi*...don't. I'm not ready to relinquish my freedom. But if you want what's best for the kingdom, we can work together behind the scenes to straighten things out without either of us being trapped in such a lofty position. You might think the throne is something to want, but believe me, what we now have is perfect. Power and the ability to do everything we want with it without being the ones everyone looks to for answers and solutions, the ones who are responsible and accountable for everything that goes on in their land."

Numair shook his head, suffocating with urgency. "I haven't made up my mind. I've just called you here to vet things out. I'm just telling you what I've come to believe lately."

"If you're still revising your stance, I hope you'll reconsider your belief about my father's guilt. I know I have no proof. I have nothing but my instincts and my lifelong knowledge of him. But if you've come to value me, I hope you'll value my judgment, too."

"Any resolution has to wait for another time, Najeeb."

"Just promise me you won't take any steps against him before we have unequivocal proof."

"I will do nothing until I get Jenan back. Only she matters to me now. Only she matters, period."

Knowing this was the most he'd get from Numair for now, Najeeb nodded. After a moment's hesitation, he extended his hand. "I'm sorry I made things worse. I hope you forgive me. I will do anything to rectify my mistake."

Even with a tornado of anxiety tearing everything up inside him, he took the proffered hand. "I was the one who started this, and I'll be the one to end it. At any price."

Before Numair withdrew his hand, Najeeb tightened his grip and dragged him closer, his eyes ablaze with sincerity. "I didn't mean what I said about Jenan earlier. She loves you, and if you love her as much, she'll believe you and in you again. She will take you back."

Numair said nothing as Najeeb turned to leave. For he'd felt how hurt Jenan had been, how pregnancy had multiplied her feeling of betrayal by a factor of a thousand. As he'd feared it would. Getting her back now felt like an impossibility.

But if he couldn't get her back, he would still pay his very life to restore her peace.

Two hours later, Numair couldn't wait anymore. One more second of inaction and he would suffer a stroke.

So he rushed to Zafrana's royal palace, all the way preparing his explanations. But he didn't find her there. The last time her family had heard from her was when she'd gone to him earlier that day.

Knowing she wouldn't answer him, he had her sisters try every method of communication. She answered none.

Out of his mind with anxiety, he sounded the general alarm to his brothers as he tore off to the States to search for her. But she seemed to have disappeared the moment she'd landed in New York, where all flights out of Zafrana landed in the States. During his flight, the men he'd sent looking for her couldn't find her anywhere she used to frequent, or couldn't even trace her steps after she left the airport.

His desperation burgeoned with every dead end, every second feeling like wading deeper in a waking nightmare.

Somewhere along the way, the nightmare metamorphosed into his old one.

But this time it was different.

Instead of men boarding his father's boat, it was tossed by waves as tall as skyscrapers. His father wrestled with a huge sail as he shouted for him to get back belowdecks before losing control of the sail that whacked him violently on the head and knocked him overboard. Then the boat capsized, tossing Numair after him.

Wrestling to the surface of the water, of the dream, his whole body discharging with sick electricity, he called Antonio and demanded that his brother meet him as soon as he landed in New York.

Antonio was there as agreed, in the limo that waited for him outside the airport. As soon as Ameen opened the door for him and he got in, Numair began to recount the searingly vivid vision.

Antonio's cool blue eyes regarded him calmly before the man exhaled. "That's what I've been hoping for, though I didn't think it a possibility it would happen spontaneously."

"What the hell do you mean?"

"I knew it would take an even more profound terror than the one you suffered when you saw your father drown and almost drowned yourself to drag more memories to the surface. When I asked for more sessions, I was going to try plunging you into an artificial panic state to dig deeper into your psyche. But since you fear nothing, I didn't know if I could even do it. But something did manage to scare you more than all the horrors in your life. Your fear for Jenan's safety and your dread you might even lose her. Those fears finally managed to jog your memories free."

"You think those were memories?"

"Not just any memories. I think these are finally your *real* memories."

"But I remembered a very different version before."

Antonio pursed his lips. "I did tell you I felt there was more to what you remembered. In hypnosis, subjects frequently take a kernel of a memory and dress it in confabulations that suit their emotional and psychological needs. You wanted someone to be responsible for your father's death, for your years of enslavement, so you invented the attackers, then used circumstantial evidence to form a perfect conspiracy that validated your alleged memories. We can do more sessions to make sure, but I'm fairly confident this is the truth at last."

Numair stared at Antonio, but saw only his realizations. He *had* needed an enemy to hold responsible, to vanquish, to pay for everything he'd lost and suffered.

But this *was* the reality at last. This was what had happened.

"I'm sorry, Phantom." Antonio looked serious when he almost never did. "As unsatisfying and unfair as I know this feels to you, it seems your father's death and your ordeal were only due to an accident."

At Antonio's unaccustomed sympathy, Numair roused himself from his musings. "No, no, it's okay."

Unconvinced by Numair's preoccupied response, Antonio pressed, "I think you should be relieved it was. This brings you closure, and rests your father in peace."

Numair nodded distractedly. Antonio *was* talking sense. But now that he'd given him a plausible explanation for the disturbing visions, the whole thing ceased to matter to him. All that mattered was that he found Jenan.

Antonio went on, "This even gives you the possibility of a family without the ugliness such a crime would have visited on all of you for generations to come."

The word *generations* hit Numair like a hammer to the

temple. For there would be a coming generation for him. It had been something he'd never truly visualized, even when there'd been every chance Jenan would get pregnant. And now she was.

But she no longer wanted to be. Not with his child.

"Phantom? Are you okay?"

At Antonio's nudging, Numair realized the rumbling sound he heard had been issuing from himself. It was a moan of agony, of regret and dread. "No, I'm not. I injured Jenan irreparably."

Antonio shrugged. "Prostrate yourself at her feet— which I'd love to see, by the way—and she'll forgive you."

"Even if she forgives me, she'll never trust me again. Or love me."

Before Antonio could respond, Numair's phone rang. A feverish glance at the caller ID made him growl as if with a kick in the gut. Richard.

The moment the line clicked, Richard's deep taunt poured into his brain. "After meeting your runaway princess, I'm considering doing her the favor of a lifetime and not telling you where she is."

Apoplectic fury took him over. Rabid threats, torrents of them, burst out of him like rapid fire.

Richard only chuckled. "Not only won't you flay me alive and all the other lovely sentiments you just expressed, you also now owe me another favor. No, scratch that. I now practically own you."

"Hang up, Richard." Numair's growl was so harsh it scraped his throat raw. "I'll find her on my own."

"Will you survive until then? And if you don't care about your suffering, would you leave her with disillusion preying on her a moment longer if you can help it?"

"Dammit, Cobra, *where is she*?" His roar made Antonio lurch and wince and Ameen almost lose control of the wheel.

"Don't give yourself a stroke, Phantom. You need your nervous system intact for crawling at her feet." Threats hurtled from Numair again before Richard interrupted. "I want a promise before I send you her location."

"What the *hell* do you want?"

"Nothing. Now. But when the time comes and I want to collect, I want one of those binding promises of yours that you'll do it without question."

"Do what?"

"Whatever I ask."

Though his head was about to explode with rage, Numair was ready to sign an actual contract that made him Richard's slave in return for immediate knowledge of Jenan's whereabouts.

"I pledge it. But say another word that isn't Jenan's location and I *will* flay you."

Richard hadn't said another word. He'd just chuckled and ended the call. The next second Numair's phone had buzzed with a text message with Jenan's address.

After dumping Antonio on the nearest curb, Numair had Ameen tearing back to his jet. He was now flying cross-country to California.

According to Richard, she'd rented a place in the desert. A year's contract had been signed. It seemed she'd wanted to escape her old life and anything that reminded her of him.

The seven and a half hours it took him to be standing on the doorstep of her rented condo in Rancho Mirage finished the last reserves of his endurance.

She opened the door, puffy eyed and precious and everything he wanted in life. He would have fallen to his knees before her if she hadn't immediately turned around, leaving him to follow her inside.

Clearly not surprised that he'd found her, she started

immediately. "I already told you you'd get what you want. You don't have to mollify me so I'd be easier to handle. I won't give you any trouble. I know no one can stop you, certainly not me, so I won't even initiate a losing fight."

"Jenan…please…"

Her deadened tone cut him off more effectively than if she'd screamed. "I'm pragmatic enough to know that whatever I wanted for my life no longer matters, and any plans or hopes I ever had are over. I have no one to blame for this but myself. I'm the one who disregarded every caution and plunged headfirst into your trap, and the result is an innocent baby, who's now the one thing that matters. I don't expect you'd be involved in its life as a regular father would, but you'll have whatever role you wish. Because I can't stop you, but mainly because I won't have the baby suffering the consequences of my folly in making you its father. I won't compound this disaster by turning its life into a battlefield over it.

"Now that you'll take over Zafrana and Saraya, you'll be there most of the time. But since you know my position on living there, we'll negotiate a schedule when I'll come periodically, so you can see your child. As long as you stay away from me, everything will be exactly as you want."

His every fiber shrieked for him to grab her, drag her back from the void of estrangement and into his heart. He could only stand before her, helpless for the first time since he was ten.

"I want nothing but for you to give me a chance to explain. What Najeeb said—"

"—is just what you told him." She spoke over him again, her lifelessness another blow to his shriveled heart. "But it isn't the truth still. I can feel it. I *always* felt you were hiding major stuff, but I deluded myself into thinking it was because they were such intensely personal and painful matters, they were unspeakable to you. I thought it would hurt you all over again if you ever had to relate them to someone. I couldn't think of trespassing on your private agonies, but I was stupid enough to keep hoping you'd one day feel enough for me, and trust me enough, to unburden yourself to me."

Suddenly, her mask of numbness started to splinter, tremors of anguish breaking through, eclipsing her fragile eyes, shaking her swollen features. "Now I know you were just hiding your identity and intentions. You never told me any truth. And you're still lying now."

With the first tear that escaped the trembling pool filling her reddened eyes, he staggered back, unable to bear the brunt of her disillusion and alienation.

"You're right. I was still lying. But no more. Though I would have given anything to never have you know the whole truth about me, I owe it to you to tell you everything."

She stumbled back, too, as if from the path of a bullet. "I'm sure you have some story you think will make me slide back into trusting you, or at least make me sympathize with your motivations and understand why you did what you did. But it's too late for that. Too late for anything."

The finality of her words felt like a mortal blow. How he remained standing, or even breathing, he had no idea.

"You already do understand why I did what I did. I wanted what I believed to be my birthright, and I always do whatever it takes to get what I want. As for making you sympathetic, there's no chance for that. The story I have to tell you—all the things you sensed me hiding—will only horrify you."

That stony distance in her eyes shredded his insides with regret. She'd once looked at him as if he was the only thing she wanted to see. Now a part of him was growing inside her, a miracle made of their essences and passion, and he was the one thing she'd rather never see again.

Exposing everything about his past—things not even his brothers knew in full—was something he'd never considered before. But he couldn't hide anything from her again. He owed her everything. The absolute truth was just the first thing among countless others that included the heart he'd grown to love her with, and the life that now meant nothing without her.

Feeling as though he was ending his own life, he told her everything. *Everything.*

It could have taken hours or only minutes to relate the horrors that had happened to him at The Organization, what he'd been forced to do, to endure, what had been done to him, what he'd been guilty of since that day he'd lost his father to what he now knew had been an accident. With every word he said, absolute shock mushroomed in her eyes.

Then he had no more horrors to relate and finally exhaled a resigned breath. "So whatever you thought I was, you now realize I'm so much worse. Far worse than anything you could even imagine."

By the time he fell silent, her body and face were shaking as if with a devastating earthquake. But it was the horror in her eyes that told him everything he'd ever feared had come to pass.

He'd scared and repelled her so completely, she'd probably risk whatever she now knew he was capable of to keep herself, and their child, away from him.

He squeezed his eyes shut on the alien feeling of defeat burning in his gut.

Knowing there was nothing to fear for or to lose anymore, he confessed what lurked in the darkest corner of his being. "I did anything I had to do to survive, and once I was free, I thought I could only remain free by destroying and conquering anyone in my path. I came here believing I'd decimate anyone who stood in the way to what I considered mine. I did intend to claim the unknown daughter of the king of Zafrana, and to use her in the same way Hassan intended to. I never considered things wouldn't go my way. I never took into account that I'd develop any feelings for you since I believed I was unequipped to feel any. Then you...happened to me.

"Everything else but you disappeared. Only you remained in my universe, a new one I never knew could exist. You melted the steel vault I built around myself. Now I am unable to seek its refuge again. I would die of exposure without you."

He finally opened his eyes and saw his devastation reflected in hers. "But you are right to reject me. Not because I betrayed you, since I didn't, but because I am what I am. You have every right to deprive me of yourself, of your love. Of our child. You should, for both of your sakes. I'm a monster. And I proved it when I hurt you—the only one who ever loved me, the only one I'll ever love."

Jenan had felt she'd known true agony when she'd thought she'd been nothing but a pawn to Numair.

But what she'd felt for her own injuries was a mere twinge compared to what she felt now for his.

Every scar on his body was the evidence of what should have broken him. But he'd only grown invincible, indomitable.

There was no doubt left in her. That was finally the whole mutilating truth. The answer to her every question and doubt.

He'd truly thought Hassan had been responsible for his father's death, for his enslavement. If anyone had ever had reason to employ subterfuge to gain his ends, it was Numair.

But there was no trace of subterfuge anymore. She just

knew it. This was everything he'd hidden from her. And she no longer had any doubt that what they'd shared had never been among the deceptions.

It had all been real.

As unthinkable as everything else had been, he loved her. As deeply and completely as she loved him. No. Far more, just as he'd said. Her love had been so fickle, she hadn't even given him the benefit of the doubt.

A lung-tearing sob of shame ripped through her.

And in the next instant she was in the haven of his arms, his feverish, trembling lips all over her face and head. Every sob that shook her seemed to rack him in agony.

"Don't do this to yourself," he whispered. "I'm not worth it."

She struggled out of his embrace, and his arms fell to his sides with a look of absolute despair. He thought she was rejecting him still.

And she pounced on him, squeezed him until she felt her arms would snap. Her tears were a deluge on his chest. "You're worth *everything*. The world isn't enough to do you justice."

It was his turn to push away so he could gape at her, incomprehension on his face. "But I thought…"

"Whatever you thought was wrong. I was only hurt because I didn't know the truth. If only you'd told me…" She stopped, wiped furiously at the flood of tears, remorse submerging her. "No, I had no excuse to behave as I did. I am the guilty one here, not you, since you had every right to keep your secret. What happened to you is so enormous, I'll live my life unable to fully grasp it all. But I loved you, and at the very first test of that love, I failed you."

He stared at her, stunned, everything inside him on full display for the first time.

Then he choked, "Loved? In the past tense."

"*Ya Ullah, no.* Every single moment in time. Even when

I thought I'd never be with you again, I knew I'd never stop loving you, yearning for you. I loved you from the first moment, and I'll love you till my very last breath."

A single tear escaped one of his eyes that had turned dark jade as he stared at her, almost panting as hard as she was. As if still afraid to let himself believe, to allow himself relief.

Then he reached out an unsteady hand to cup her cheek. "I need you to understand one thing. Then you can make this declaration again once you've heard it. I wasn't exaggerating. After a lifetime of emotional deep freeze, you've decimated all my barriers and hurled me into an inferno, one I need to burn in for the rest of my life. I will love you single-mindedly, *ferociously*…till *my* very last breath."

She hurled herself at him again, rained tears and kisses all over every part of him she could reach. "Yes, yes, please, love me just like that. It's how I love you…" Her heart twisted again. "Even though I don't deserve you."

He hauled her off the ground and crashed his lips over hers, swallowing her contrition and self-blame.

By the time he raised his head, hers was spinning, her body racked with the wildfire of reclamation and her soul with the grief of agony and guilt.

"Never shed any more tears for anything if you love me, *ya hayati, ya galbi*. You are my life and my heart. When I thought I lost you, I thought my life was over. But it has all turned out for the best. This way we've found each other in spite of everything, making what we have all that more unique and unstoppable. It was even my despair over your rejection then disappearance that drove me to finally remember the vital memory that exonerated Hassan and put my demons to rest at last."

She pulled him down to her for another frenzied kiss before she could reply, "So you really do believe it was an accident."

"Yes." His gorgeous lips suddenly quirked. "Now after I was about to puree Hassan, I might even tolerate him for Najeeb and his siblings' sake. You see, because of you I've learned how to compromise. Now that will allow us to have an extended family for our baby."

The way he said *our baby* skewered through her heart with poignancy, made her legs give out.

He cursed and swung her up in his arms, homing in, unerringly as always, on her bedroom.

What followed felt like a resurrection. A surrender of everything she was. And a possession of everything he was. A merging.

Then it was next evening, and he was starting to rocket her to the most decadent reaches of ecstasy again when she finally stopped his fondling hands, needing to say something coherent for a change.

"Numair, about the baby…"

He immediately frowned, his eyes turning wary once more. She was suddenly quivering with uncertainty again.

"You said you wanted an heir…but I have a feeling it's a girl. Don't ask me how I know—"

His lips stopped her agitated words. "I wish it *is* a girl. I lived all my life among rough, gruff XY creatures, and now I want to spend the rest of my life wallowing in the delights of female companionship."

"Really?"

"Really. I will only ever tell you the whole truth from now on."

She grimaced. "Uh…sometimes the truth isn't such a great thing to hear. Like when my nose blows up to double its current size with pregnancy hormones."

He tugged lovingly on a thick tress as he suckled a breast ripening more every day with those hormones. She was still deliciously sore from his nightlong ministrations.

"Don't they believe in the region this only happens when you're carrying a boy?"

"You've done your homework *very* thoroughly." She moaned with pleasure, then stabbed her fingers in his now loose hair, making him relinquish her nipple before she lost whatever was left of her mind again. She needed to say something else. "About Zafrana's throne…"

He lowered his mouth to her flesh again, skimmed his way up to her lips, his smile filling her with joy. "I have no more desire to take over my heritage. The only thing I care about now is the future we'll make together for our children."

"Children!"

"Only as many—or as few—as you like," he rushed to assure her. "This baby is all I need. *You* are all I need."

She groaned with yet another surge of emotion. "You are all I need, too. And I want everything possible with you, and as many children as you want. But let's just take one child at a time. Let me work on this one first."

He laughed and hugged her exuberantly. "We'll work on this one, and everything else, together."

As he lowered his head and began ridding her of her last shreds of sanity, she squirmed, making him stop again. "But you *have* to claim your heritage. It would be the best thing to ever happen to Zafrana and Saraya if you merged them and sat on their combined throne."

Nipping her lower lip, he murmured, "I only want to be on the throne of your heart."

"You've been there from day one," she moaned. "And you're now stuck there."

His chuckle filled her every cell with well-being as he slid his body over hers, setting her every nerve on renewed fire. "Now to make sure I am *fused* there."

Crying out as he entered her, merged them, she again

tugged on his hair before everything but him and those carnally emotional moments ceased to matter.

"Numair…please…" Drowning in sensation, she clamped her legs around his muscled hips to stop him from tipping her into oblivion. "Promise me you will. You'll make the best king for our region as well as for my heart."

He rose above her, his eyes a conflagration of love and devotion. "I might reconsider…if you do something for me."

She nodded frantically, losing the fight, starting to undulate beneath him, the pleasure so intense it was nearly blinding. "Anything. I'll do anything for you. I'll spend my life trying to erase everything you suffered."

The ferocity he'd promised her blazed in his eyes as he thrust hard, impaling her to her very center. "You already have. Just being you, just loving me against all odds. And now you have to promise me you'll make up for the fright and desperation you caused me when you disappeared."

"Whatever you want, it's yours."

"I want you to forever let me shower you and our family with my pampering and protection, my devotion and adoration."

She arched into him as he punctuated each phrase with a thrust until he splintered her into a soul-searing orgasm.

Long after he'd joined her in the depths of bliss, she belatedly and euphorically murmured, "Done."

* * * * *

If you loved PREGNANT BY THE SHEIKH,
pick up the other stories in
THE BILLIONAIRES OF BLACK CASTLE *series*
from USA TODAY *bestselling author Olivia Gates*

FROM ENEMY'S DAUGHTER
TO EXPECTANT BRIDE and
SCANDALOUSLY EXPECTING HIS CHILD

Available now from Harlequin Desire!

If you're on Twitter, tell us what you think of
Harlequin Desire! #harlequindesire

REQUEST YOUR FREE BOOKS!
2 FREE NOVELS PLUS 2 FREE GIFTS!

ALWAYS POWERFUL, PASSIONATE AND PROVOCATIVE

YES! Please send me 2 FREE Harlequin Desire® novels and my 2 FREE gifts (gifts are worth about $10). After receiving them, if I don't wish to receive any more books, I can return the shipping statement marked "cancel." If I don't cancel, I will receive 6 brand-new novels every month and be billed just $4.55 per book in the U.S. or $4.99 per book in Canada. That's a savings of at least 13% off the cover price! It's quite a bargain! Shipping and handling is just 50¢ per book in the U.S. and 75¢ per book in Canada.* I understand that accepting the 2 free books and gifts places me under no obligation to buy anything. I can always return a shipment and cancel at any time. Even if I never buy another book, the two free books and gifts are mine to keep forever.

225/326 HDN F4ZC

Name	(PLEASE PRINT)	
Address		Apt. #
City	State/Prov.	Zip/Postal Code

Signature (if under 18, a parent or guardian must sign)

Mail to the **Harlequin® Reader Service:**
IN U.S.A.: P.O. Box 1867, Buffalo, NY 14240-1867
IN CANADA: P.O. Box 609, Fort Erie, Ontario L2A 5X3

Want to try two free books from another line?
Call 1-800-873-8635 or visit www.ReaderService.com.

* Terms and prices subject to change without notice. Prices do not include applicable taxes. Sales tax applicable in N.Y. Canadian residents will be charged applicable taxes. Offer not valid in Quebec. This offer is limited to one order per household. Not valid for current subscribers to Harlequin Desire books. All orders subject to credit approval. Credit or debit balances in a customer's account(s) may be offset by any other outstanding balance owed by or to the customer. Please allow 4 to 6 weeks for delivery. Offer available while quantities last.

Your Privacy—The Harlequin® Reader Service is committed to protecting your privacy. Our Privacy Policy is available online at www.ReaderService.com or upon request from the Harlequin Reader Service.

We make a portion of our mailing list available to reputable third parties that offer products we believe may interest you. If you prefer that we not exchange your name with third parties, or if you wish to clarify or modify your communication preferences, please visit us at www.ReaderService.com/consumerschoice or write to us at Harlequin Reader Service Preference Service, P.O. Box 9062, Buffalo, NY 14269. Include your complete name and address.

HD13R

Disowned and pregnant after one passionate night in Vegas, Cassidy Corelli shows up on the doorstep of the only man who can help her...

Read on for a sneak peek at
TWINS ON THE WAY,
the latest in USA TODAY *bestselling author*
Janice Maynard's
THE KAVANAGHS OF SILVER GLEN *series.*

Without warning, Gavin stood up. Suddenly the office shrank in size. His personality and masculine presence sucked up all the available oxygen. Pacing so near Cassidy's chair that he almost brushed her knees, Gavin shot her a look laden with frustration. "We need some ground rules if you're going to stay with me while we sort out this pregnancy, Cassidy. First of all, we're going to forget that we've ever seen each other naked."

She gulped, fixating on the dusting of hair where the shallow V-neck of his sweater revealed a peek of his chest. "I'm pretty sure that's going to be the elephant in the room. Our night in Vegas was amazing. Maybe not for you, but for me. Telling me to forget it is next to impossible."

"Good Lord, woman. Don't you have any social armor, at all?"

"I am not a liar. If you want me to pretend we haven't been intimate, I'll try, but I make no promises."

He leaned over her, resting his hands on the arms of the chair. His beautifully sculpted lips were in kissing distance. Smoke-colored irises filled with turbulent emotions locked on hers like lasers. "I may be attracted to you, Cass, but I don't completely trust you. It's too soon. So, despite evidence to the contrary, I do have some self-control."

Maybe *he* did, but hers was melting like snow in the hot sun. His coffee-scented breath brushed her cheek. This close, she could see tiny crinkles at the corners of his eyes. She might have called them laugh lines if she could imagine her onetime lover being lighthearted enough and smiling long enough to create them.

"You're crowding my personal space," she said primly.

For several seconds, she was sure he was going to steal a kiss. Her breathing went shallow, her nipples tightened and a tumultuous feeling rose in her chest. Something volatile. For the first time, she understood that whatever madness had taken hold of them in Las Vegas was neither a fluke nor a solitary event.

Don't miss
TWINS ON THE WAY
by USA TODAY *bestselling author Janice Maynard.*

Available April 2015,
wherever Harlequin® Desire books and ebooks are sold.

www.Harlequin.com

Love the Harlequin book you just read?

Your opinion matters.

Review this book on your favorite book site, review site, blog or your own social media properties and share your opinion with other readers!

Be sure to connect with us at:
Harlequin.com/Newsletters
Facebook.com/HarlequinBooks
Twitter.com/HarlequinBooks

JUST CAN'T GET ENOUGH?

Join our social communities
and talk to us online.

You will have access to the latest
news on upcoming titles and special
promotions, but most importantly,
you can talk to other fans about your
favorite Harlequin reads.

Harlequin.com/Community

Facebook.com/HarlequinBooks

Twitter.com/HarlequinBooks

Pinterest.com/HarlequinBooks

**Stay up-to-date on all your
romance-reading news with the
Harlequin Shopping Guide,
featuring bestselling authors, exciting new
miniseries, books to watch and more!**

The newest issue will be delivered right to you
with our compliments! There are 4 each year.

Signing up is easy.

EMAIL

ShoppingGuide@Harlequin.ca

WRITE TO US

HARLEQUIN BOOKS
Attention: Customer Service Department
P.O. Box 9057, Buffalo, NY 14269-9057

OR PHONE

1-800-873-8635 in the United States
1-888-343-9777 in Canada

Please allow 4-6 weeks for delivery of the first issue by mail.